No Luck for Lincoln

No Luck for Lincoln

Helen B. Walters

Illustrated by Lloyd Ostendorf

Abingdon   Nashville

NO LUCK FOR LINCOLN

Library of Congress Cataloging in Publication Data

Walters, Helen B.
  No luck for Lincoln
  Bibliography: p.
  SUMMARY: Portrays incidents in the childhood of Abe
Lincoln that were related either by Lincoln or his early friends.
    1. Lincoln, Abraham, Pres. U.S., 1809-1865--Child-
hood and youth--Juvenile literature. 2. Presidents--United
States--Biography--Juvenile literature
  [1. Lincoln, Abraham, Pres. U.S., 1809-1865--Childhood
and youth. 2. Presidents] I. Title.
E457.905.W34   973.7'092'4   [B]   [92]   80-27164

ISBN 0-687-28030-3

Manufactured in the United States of America

TO
JULIE, SKIP, AND ADAM

Contents

Foreword

The dates of Abe's boyhood are uncertain. None of his neighbors thought the Lincoln family important enough to try to record what its members did. The few records kept were dates put into a Bible.

Abe went to school about a year, a few weeks at a time. He could attend a class only when he was not needed for work at home.

In this book I have taken the few incidents told either by Lincoln or his early friends and put them into the setting of that era.

CHAPTER 1

Something's Wrong

Y ou young-uns stay outside," thundered a big
man standing at the entrance to a log cabin. He
shook a thick finger at Abe and Sarah. "No hanging
around this doorway." He stepped backward into the
room and closed the door.

The two children stood in the Kentucky sunshine,
their gray eyes wide in alarm. Never had their father
acted so upset. What was going on inside their cabin?
The mystery had started at sun-up when a neighbor,
Aunt Peggy Peabody, rode up the road in a great
hurry. At once the children were told to play outdoors.

Sarah twisted her two braids. "With the door closed
it must be powerful dark inside."

Her younger brother nodded. Both knew that the
only light in the room came from either the big fireplace
or from the doorway. The cabin had no windows cut
into its log walls.

Young Abe rumpled his black hair with fingers that

had not touched soap or water for some time. It was as if the grown-ups were too busy to worry about a three-year-old.

"I reckon we can't go in 'cause Ma's sick," Sarah said.

She kicked her feet through red and gold leaves as she went over to a log that Pa had started to split for rails. Her brother joined her, and they both sat down. They were dressed alike in linsey-woolsey shirts that hung to their knees.

For some minutes they leaned together and shivered. The afternoon sun tried to brighten the clearing in front of the cabin.

Both Abe and Sarah cocked their heads trying to hear the sounds in the cabin. They could hear somebody moaning. Occasionally they heard the crackling of Ma's new cornhusk mattress. As moments passed the wind turned colder, and they burrowed their feet deeper under the leaves. Then suddenly they jerked to attention. Their father strode through the doorway swinging a pail. He went straight to fill it from a barrel that caught rainwater from the roof. Then he hurried inside.

"Why do they need more water?" asked Sarah.

Abe shook his head.

When the sun sank behind the treetops the children edged together for warmth. Finally, Sarah broke the silence.

"If we lay on our stomachs in the leaves, we'll be warmer."

In a moment they snuggled into the leaves and listened. They heard their father drag a log over the hard trampled dirt floor in the cabin and throw it into the fireplace. A shower of sparks burst up the stone chimney. From under the crack below the door they saw the shadows of Aunt Peggy's skirts swing back and forth to the corner bed.

Minutes dragged along. The sun dropped lower allowing shadows from the forest to creep over the clearing. As if for safety both children wiggled deeper into the leaves, still straining to peer under the door. It became easier after somebody lighted a lamp, which was only a wick in a cup of bear grease. The flame flickered and gave the impression of black ghosts jumping around the room.

Without warning the door opened and Father walked out swinging another pail. But now something was different. His step had a new bounce as he came toward them. His generous mouth stretched into a broad grin as he planted his big body in front of them.

"The Lord has smiled on us." His calloused fingers stroked his black beard in an awkward gesture of tenderness. "He give you young-uns a new brother. Yep! He be Thomas Lincoln the second."

"New brother?" puzzled Abe. "Not see him come."

"He be a baby," explained Sarah with the wisdom of her five years. "Can we see him?"

"Not yet." The father glanced toward a dark cloud churning in the sky. "It be fixin' to rain."

"It feels more like snowing," said Sarah, her teeth chattering.

"Well, rain or snow, tonight we have a jolly-up. The Lord don't give every man a second son."

"Popcorn?" Abe asked, getting to his feet.

"Yep. Have hot cider, too. And a bit of maple sugar."

Abe clapped his hands and bounced on his toes.

"Here!" Tom Lincoln held out the pail. "You young-uns gather the eggs. Be sure you put all the chickens in the coops. I seen fox tracks around."

"Yes, Pa." Sarah took the pail.

"Move fast. I go fetch up the cow. Reckon I got to milk her myself." He wagged his head in disgust for milking was in his mind a woman's work. He turned toward the barn, and the children started for the hen house.

Before anyone had taken more than a few steps the door opened again and out hustled a gaunt woman wiping her hands on an apron. Her white hair revealed her years and the lines in her face told that she had met and conquered many crises of pioneer living. Everybody depended on Aunt Peggy Peabody.

"Brother Lincoln!" She strode forward, her skirts

15

fluttering on each side like frightened wings. "Sir!" She halted in front of him. "I got to tell you the truth. I no can save him." She planted her hands on her hips in a manner of finality.

"Not save him?" exploded the new father. "You got to!"

"Sir, he be powerful weak."

"My son looked perfect to me."

"It be his breathing. Something's wrong. What, I don't rightly know. I be no doctor."

"Doctor?" Tom glanced toward the road which was little more than a trail. The nearest doctor was miles away and he had no wagon. Tom turned to stare at Aunt Peggy. Her words made no sense. She was rated the best granny woman in Kentucky. She had delivered dozens of babies, and folks said she never lost a one. Why, she had even brought Abe into the world. And now she could not save the new baby. Surely this was a nightmare. After a moment he jerked up as if fresh pioneer blood surged through his arteries.

"Ma'am, my baby be going to live. We pray for him tonight at evening prayers. The Lord will save little Thomas."

Aunt Peggy shook her head. "He ain't gonna make it." She turned and retreated to the warm cabin.

"My son will live," Tom called after her.

CHAPTER 2

Night of Mystery

B y the time Abe and Sarah entered the cabin twilight had quieted the land with a drizzle. Aunt Peggy was stirring a big kettle of burgoo, a stew made of venison and vegetables. The aroma of herbs filled the room and both children licked their lips.

Sarah put the bucket of eggs on the table, and Abe tiptoed to stand in awe beside the bed in the corner. His mother's face looked whiter than he had ever seen it. She turned her head on the pillow and smiled at him. Beside her cheek lay a tiny face even whiter than hers. Because the baby's eyes were closed Abe lowered his voice to a whisper.

"He have popcorn?"

"He has no teeth, dear."

"No teeth?" Abe bent to study the small face.

Just then Tom Lincoln came through the doorway with a pail.

"Here be rich milk to make you better," he told

17

Nancy. "I hope it don't thunder and sour it." He put the pail on a bench.

"Supper be ready," announced Aunt Peggy picking up a ladle. "Get your bowls."

Each child took a bowl from the shelf and held it for her to fill. Then they took their places at the table. In a moment their father joined them.

"Bow your heads!" he ordered. "Close your eyes!"

They obeyed and as usual he began a long grace. Abe fidgeted and sniffed the pungent odor of the stew under his nose. When at last came the "amen," he picked up a spoon and began to eat. The sound of slurping blended in with the wind whistling through cracks between the logs of the cabin walls. At last the meal ended.

"Now popcorn?" asked Abe.

His father arose. "I promised, didn't I? A Lincoln always keeps his word."

He dropped a handful of kernels into an iron pot, slammed on a lid and put it on the hearth. Soon there came a sound of popping. Each child sat on a three-legged stool and munched the fluffy corn. Wind howled and the fireplace log not only crackled but sent sparks into the room. Suddenly a new sound caused everybody to twist toward the door.

"That be wolves," whispered Sarah in a trembling tone.

Tom Lincoln jumped to his feet and for a sharp

moment studied the door. Surely a pack couldn't push it open. To make sure he shoved a bench across the entrance.

"There!" He dusted his hands. "We be safe." He lifted a Bible from a box and sat down at an angle so that the firelight fell over the pages. "Now we have family prayers and pray for little Thomas."

Both children tried to listen as he pretended to read. Abe's eyelids would not stay open and in the middle of prayer he fell off his stool. With a jolt he scrambled to his feet and looked to see if he would be whipped. Instead of reaching for his rod Father wagged a finger at both children.

"Off to bed!"

"Where'll me and Abe sleep?" Sarah pointed to a damp spot in their corner of the room.

"Mmmmm. You can bed down in front of the hearth. Aunt Peggy will sleep on the bed with Ma."

Abe and Sarah exchanged glances of delight. It was fun to sleep in front of the warm coals after Pa banked them with ashes to keep them alive till morning. Each child unrolled a cornhusk mattress and started to lie down.

"First say good night to your new brother. And to Ma," said their father.

Abe and Sarah padded across to the bed where little Thomas lay wrapped in a piece of wool blanket. Aunt Peggy stood at the side of the bed as if ready for some mysterious action. She patted Abe's shoulder and spoke in a low tone.

"Say good-bye till ye meet in heaven."

"I heard that," bristled Tom Lincoln. Then to Abe in a voice of command. "Say good night!"

"Good night," whispered Abe.

"Good night," added Sarah.

They kissed their mother then walked to the hearth and sank onto their mattresses. Their father spread a deerhide over Abe and made sure Sarah was covered.

Abe watched his father toss a buffalo hide onto the floor and lie down facing the doorway. All would be well as long as Pa was near. The room settled into dimness with the only light a glow from the hearth. Gradually the sound of snoring blended into the noise of distant howling of wolves. Pa was asleep. Slowly Abe's eyelids closed.

The next morning when Abe awakened, he saw that the door had been hooked back to let in the sunshine. His mother sat in her rocker looking pale and sad. Aunt Peggy was packing her things to leave.

"Where's the baby?" The boy looked around as if sensing something unusual.

"He went back to heaven, dear," replied his mother, a strange catch in her voice. "Your breakfast be on the table."

20

No Luck for Lincoln

Abe frowned at the usual corn dodger and mug of milk then turned toward the bed. It was empty.

His mother wiped her eyes then spoke, once again, this time in a husky whisper.

"The baby went back to heaven."

"Heaven?" Abe thought for a moment and his face brightened. According to what he had heard at a church camp meeting heaven was a fine place with angels to play with. "Back to heaven," he repeated. "Not see him go."

"You were asleep, dear."

Abe nodded. "Where Pa?"

"He may be in the barn or maybe gone up the hill." When Abe started out the door she went on. "You wait here. Eat your breakfast"

As Abe sat down at the table his father appeared. He carried a boulder about the shape of a small pumpkin. Nancy Lincoln's eyes followed him as he set the rock on the hearth. Then he turned to her and nodded as if to say that it was done. She wiped her eyes as he spoke.

"God giveth and he seen fitten to take away."

Abe got to his feet. "Take away brother? We get new one? With teeth?"

Tom made no reply. Instead, his eyes measured the size of his son. "I be glad when you get big enough to help me with the chores." Then to Nancy. "When is this boy going to wear man-pants instead of that silly shirt you keep on him? It make him look like a girl."

"All boys wear those shirts until . . ."

"I want Abe put into pants. It'll make him look older."

"Tom! I can't make pants till you buy me a needle. The thorns I been using ain't strong enough to go through deerhide."

Tom whirled around and strode out the doorway.

That evening after prayers Nancy slumped in her rocker. Tom sat astride a bench with the boulder in front of him. On it he was chipping something. Abe watched. Finally he spoke.

"Pa, what that?"

"To mark the grave of Thomas Lincoln. Tomorrow I mean to learn you to chip on this. You got to learn to work. All life be work."

"Not just work." Nancy lifted her chin. "Abe and Sarah be going to learn readin' and writin'. Aunt Peggy said a school be startin' soon. Maybe Abe be big enough to get in."

"Nonsense. All he needs to know is how to use tools. I can learn him that."

For a long time Abe listened to the pounding on the grave marker and studied his fathers powerful body. Everybody liked Tom Lincoln. If he said school was a silly place for a boy then it was. Let Sarah learn readin' and writin'. He was going to be like his father. Yep, he was. Then into his thoughts came his mother's voice so low she seemed to be talking to the squeak of her rocker.

"My son be agoin' to school. Yep, he be."

CHAPTER 3

Noises in the Dark

T he next evening when Tom brought in the pail of milk he was worried.

"A devil's howler be coming."

Abe sneaked across the room to peek out the door. By the light from the room he saw iridescent eyes peering from low bushes.

"Get away from that door!" ordered his father. "Anything can happen tonight."

Abe returned to sit on a stool while Sarah did the dishes.

"Pa!" Sarah's voice trembled when she joined them. "Can wolves get into our barn?"

"Them varmints can get in most anywhere."

Abe and Sarah looked at each other, alarm plain on their faces.

After a moment she went on. "Could they get Ham and Bacon?"

"I got bigger worries than a couple little pigs."

25

No Luck for Lincoln

"They be our pets." Abe stiffened.

"I got worry over the cow and Old Limpy." Tom lowered his body onto a stool. "If it weren't for leaving you all unprotected I'd go sleep in the barn."

After a short time the wind began to blow with violence. It drove rain between the logs of the walls. Abe and Sarah tried to stuff the cracks with bits of moss and shavings from the kindling box. Branches whacked against the walls. Acorns hit the roof like rocks.

"We all be warmer in bed," their father finally said. "I keep the fire going. Put your mattresses in front of the hearth."

Abe lay down and pulled a deerhide blanket over his head to shut out the scary sounds. At last weariness closed his eyes.

On awakening in the morning he bounded to the doorway. What he saw tightened a band of terror around his stomach. He called his sister.

"Yep, them be bear tracks," she said. "I hope they didn't get into the barn."

By noon the rain turned to snow. Tom shook off the flakes when he came from the barn for a hot noon meal.

"You young-uns can help me in the barn this afternoon," he said, putting down a pail of eggs.

Abe and Sarah grinned in delight.

By dusk their work in the barn was finished, and the three ran up the path to the cabin.

Noises in the Dark

"Not much milk," Tom announced, putting a pail on a bench. "All the animals be nervous."

"Tom!" Nancy stiffened in alarm. "If we get snowed in be there enough food for them?"

"Sure."

"And for us, too?"

"Don't worry none."

That evening wind rushed down the chimney, threatening to blow out the hearth log. A sheet of snow loosened on the roof and fell with an eerie plop. The family soon went to bed.

The next afternoon Tom bundled up to return to the barn and then turned to his son.

"Abe, you be big enough to help me while Sarah churns. Put on your shoes and come along."

To Abe, escaping to the barn was a spree.

"Ham and Bacon growed," he announced, petting them.

"Why not? All they do is eat. Take care you don't fall with that bucket of eggs. Ma needs some for supper."

Abe moved warily up the path. Nearing the cabin he paused to stare at the icicles hanging from the edge of the roof.

After the evening meal Tom set his gun beside the doorway. As if to answer the mute question on his son's face he explained.

"Wild critters may try to get into the barn. If I hear a noise tonight I'll go after them."

27

No Luck for Lincoln

After evening prayers the family sat warming themselves at the fireplace. Gradually the outside world hushed until it was almost spooky. Tom flung an extra log into the flames.

"Off to bed!" he ordered. "You young-uns sleep in your clothes tonight."

Abe had scarcely closed his eyes when he was jerked awake by a racket coming from the barn. He sat up. The cow bawled; the pigs squealed; Old Limpy kicked against her stall. He saw his father leap from bed to grab his rifle.

Abe rolled to his feet and hustled to the doorway. Sarah joined him. The moon shone overhead like a polished pewter saucer. For a bewildering moment Abe saw his father's dark figure on the path. Then came more agonized squealing.

"That be Ham and Bacon," cried Sarah.

A shot echoed through the woods. Abe saw his father standing with a rifle at his shoulder. Two huge figures were waddling across the meadow toward the safety of trees.

"Be them bears?" called Sarah as Pa came to the cabin.

"Yep."

"You scared them off," she replied with relief.

"Not soon enough. They got Ham and Bacon."

Abe tried to speak but only a choking sound came out. His whole body sagged.

"Now don't start blubbering!" ordered his father, coming to the doorway. "Soon I ride over to neighbors and maybe swap some pumpkins for a couple more shoats."

"They be not Ham and Bacon," Sarah sniffled.

"There be no law agin giving them the same names. Quit being a baby. The Good Book says we got to be strong. Go inside where it be warm."

"Ain't you coming, too?" she asked.

"Nope. I sleep in the barn the rest of the night."

"I stay with you?" begged Abe.

"Nope. You look after your Ma and sister. Shut the door to keep in the heat."

CHAPTER 4

Swap
for Man-Pants

S pring came early as if to make up for the harsh
winter. Crickets chirped in gratitude. Millions of
flies hatched in the rotting canes and winged straight to
the Lincoln's barnyard. Mosquitoes added their songs
and fireflies darted at night.

Trees decorated their branches with bright leaves
and the moist ground pushed up purple violets. Abe
watched a pair of robins repairing an old nest.
Overhead passenger pigeons darkened the sky as they
wheeled to their nesting woods. The whole world
seemed excited. Surely something good was going to
happen.

One morning Abe helped his father sling a bag of
tools onto the back of Old Limpy. Then his father
mounted her.

"Off to split rails," Pa announced. "You and Sarah
do good chores and I may bring you something." With
a wave he left.

Swap for Man-Pants

All morning Abe listened. At noon he heard the limping gait of the aged horse and ran to greet his father.

"You bring it, Pa?"

"Yep." Grinning broadly, Tom Lincoln dismounted. From his saddlebag he lifted a squealing little pig. "Here!" He handed it to his son. "And here be one for your sister."

"They pretties." Abe tried to hold both squirming animals as he started for the cabin doorway.

Tom followed and as he walked he studied his lanky son. Gradually the father's brows pulled together in a scowl and his jaw set in a stern line. Inside the cabin he waited until Ma had seen the little pigs then he spoke, a sharp edge in his tone.

"Nancy! Have you looked at our son of late?"

"Of course, Why?"

"He's growed. His shirt be too short."

"I know that." She stiffened.

"He be too big to wear one of Sarah's dresses for a shirt. I want to take him with me as a carpenter's helper but I can't take nobody who looks like a girl. He needs man-pants."

"Tom Lincoln!" Nancy shook a finger at him. "I told you plenty times I make him man-pants when you get me deerhide and steel needles."

"I get them soon as I ride to Elizabethtown."

Abe's mouth stretched in a wide grin. At last he

would not have to wear a dress for a shirt. All the boys he saw walking along the Cumberland Road wore pants. Now it was his turn. Above the excited thumping of his heart he heard his father speak.

"Son, take your shoat to the barn. Then meet me in the low field. Me and you is gonna plant."

"Yes, sir."

Abe joined his father but could not keep his mind on his job. There was too much moving along the Cumberland Road that ran by the edge of their farm. Boys in pants walked beside oxen pulling covered wagons. Then suddenly he spied something different. Among the rough wagons rolled a shiny black thing with only two large wheels. It was pulled by a pair of prancing white horses.

"Pa, look! What that?"

Tom wrinkled his nose. "They call it a shay."

"Who in it?"

"Most likely a dandy from a town called Washington."

"We go there? Have shay?"

"Naw. That be not for such as us. We got to work."

As the afternoon wore on Abe blinked at another sight. A line of men, women, and boys were clomping along with their ankles chained to one another. He could hear the clanking of the links. Never, never had he seen faces tanned by the sun till they turned black.

"Look, Pa! Who them?"

"Slaves." His father made a gesture of spitting to show his disgust. "That white man aridin' behind them be takin' them to market to sell, every God's soul of them."

"Even the boys?"

"Yep. Sell 'em like calves."

Abe gasped. "Be that right?"

"Nope."

"Then why . . . ?"

"Son, morals round here be powerful low. I want to move."

"Where to, Pa?"

"Your Uncle Thomas Sparrow told me there be government acres dirt-cheap in Indiana. And I can get an honest title to land. Yep! I may quit this Sodom-and-Gomorrah country."

"Where Indiana?" The boy's eyes sparkled with an inherited love of adventure.

"Down the road. Across the Ohio River."

Abe said no more yet he sneaked glances at the Cumberland Road. In his mind he saw his family traveling there. But before he went he needed pants. He must find a way to get them.

Abe was extra strong for his four years and his father gave him more chores. He carried water, cleaned ashes from the hearth, and fed hay to the animals. He learned to use a small hatchet to chop kindling for the wood box.

No Luck for Lincoln

Each morning Abe helped his father load the bag of carpentry tools onto old Limpy and wave as his father rode away. Ma claimed that Pa was the best carpenter in all Kentucky. That always made Abe beam with pride. He would learn to be like his father. Yep he would. Just as soon as he got man-pants.

One noon Abe was filling the trough with water for the animals when he heard hoofs coming up the trail from the road. Surprised that his father would come back so early, Abe ran to see what was wrong. Instead of his father he saw a stranger dressed in buckskin breeches and a fringed jacket. He carried no rifle but led a mule that was wide with two baskets stuffed with an assortment of objects. Abe blinked in surprise. Strangers never came to their cabin. Something had happened to Pa. Abe ran and met the man in the clearing in front of the cabin.

"Howdy, Missy," the man greeted Abe.

"I be no missy, sir." Anger seethed red up Abe's throat.

"No?" The man's gaze lingered on the boy's shirt. "My mistake. Go tell your Maw I got things she wants."

Abe turned but before he took a step his mother appeared, followed by Sarah.

"Morning, Ma'am. I be Peter Peddler." He bent in a gallant bow. "No doubt ye heard of me."

"Can't say as I have, sir."

"Well, ma'am, I got wares ye can't live without."

34

"We live without a powerful lot," she replied.

"How about a big iron spider?" From a basket he drew out a heavy iron skillet with a lid.

"Got one. But there be one thing I need. Needles. Yes, and deerhide for my boy's pants."

"I got both. But they ain't cheap." He handed the needles to Nancy and the deerhide to Abe. "Now!" He rubbed his palms together. "What ye got to swap?"

Abe and Nancy exchanged glances. The Lincoln family had no surplus of anything. They used up everything the farm produced. Their maple trees gave syrup, the cow provided milk, and the chickens laid eggs. Abe shifted as an idea exploded in his mind. What about his little pig? It did nothing but eat. He rumpled his hair. Should he trade a pet for a deerskin? Much as he wanted man-pants that was a hard deal. After a miserable moment he spoke in a low voice.

"Sir, you take little pig?"

The peddler shook his head. "Can't carry it."

Abe's mouth stretched in a grin of relief.

"Maybe a fat hen?" asked Sarah.

When the peddler frowned in doubt Nancy spoke up.

"Two hens plus a jar of wild honey."

"Now ye touched my weak spot. We got a deal."

Sarah and Abe brought the chickens from the barn and tied their legs together so they could not escape. These were nested in one basket and the jar of sweets put into the other. Then after giving another bow, Peter Peddler led his mule back to the main road. Not until he was out of sight did anyone speak. Abe broke the silence.

"When I get man-pants?"

"I start on them right now."

Abe clapped his hands. At last he was going to look like a boy not a missy. He could go to work with Pa. And earn money. How exciting. Then he would buy a lot of things for Ma. And after he learned to use carpenter tools real good he'd build her a shay. She could go to that wonderful town called Washington. He might even ride with her. He chuckled at the idea.

CHAPTER 5

A Broken Wagon

With so much spring and summer work to do Abe's mother did not finish his pants until autumn.

To celebrate the harvesttime feast Abe put on his first man-pants. He also wore one of his father's shirts cut down to his size. His face beamed.

Tom looked at his son and frowned. "Them pants be too short. Should come to his ankles. Not just half way down his shanks."

"That be all the leather I had," explained Nancy.

But Abe did not mind the length. He looked like a boy.

"Pa," he said, "tomorrow I go on job?"

"I try you out."

At dawn Abe rode off behind his father on Old Limpy. At sunset Tom collected not only his own pay but twelve cents for his son's help. Abe grinned. He was earning money like his father. They rode home in the frosty twilight.

A Broken Wagon

For days Abe dreamed of the things he meant to buy for his mother when Pa paid him. But a week passed and the money still stayed in the big man's pocket. Finally, one evening in December as Abe sat by the fireside shelling corn he decided to ask.

"Pa, when I get pay?"

"Till you turn twenty-one all you earn belongs to me who feeds and clothes you."

Abe gasped. "The Good Book say that?"

"Not in them words. It says a son shall honor his Pa."

Abe's lower lip rolled out in rebellion. Hot words burned on his tongue. Though he glowered at his father no sound came out. Nobody won an argument with the powerful Tom Lincoln.

A mild winter passed. By spring more and more people were moving into Kentucky along the Cumberland Road. They brought slaves to do their work. That meant it was harder for Tom to find jobs. He rode from farm to farm and grew discouraged.

One morning in late August Abe and his father were cleaning the barn. As the boy curried Old Limpy he happened to glance toward the road. A woman and two girls were walking up the lane to the Lincoln cabin.

"Pa, somebody coming."

Tom looked. "Maybe their wagon broke down." He hurried to the lane with Abe at his heels.

No Luck for Lincoln

"Morning, sir," called a woman in a blue sunbonnet. "My wagon pole is cracked."

"I fix it for you," replied Tom.

"I can pay you."

"No pay, ma'am. Helping a lady be the Christian thing. While I work you folks go in and talk to my missus. She gets powerful lonely."

Pa motioned for Abe to take them to the cabin as he headed for the barn to get his tools.

When the group entered the room, Nancy looked up from stirring a kettle of stew. The two women greeted each other while Abe brought stools for all to sit down. The guest explained that she was taking her girls to live with an uncle.

"Then they can go to school," she said.

"School?" Nancy's eyes flashed. "Where? When?"

"Starts next week in the old schoolhouse on the Allen farm. Schoolmaster Riney is teaching cipherin.'"

"Praise be!" Nancy looked toward heaven. "My prayer be answered. Now my young-uns can get some learnin'. How much do this school cost?"

"Whatever a body can pay."

"We pay something. Yep, we will."

The sunshine coming in the doorway announced that it was noon and Nancy arose.

"We all have stew. We got plenty."

A Broken Wagon

"Can I help?" asked the guest. When Nancy shook her head the woman went on. "Then I read to the young-uns."

"Can you read?" gasped Abe.

"A little." From her skirt pocket she drew out a worn book and began turning the pages. "Here's a yarn about a cat and a passel of mice."

The four children sat in a circle about her and she began to read, her calloused finger underlining each sentence. After she finished the story all hands clapped. Abe went over to examine the book. He turned the pages slowly.

"Ma'am that be a powerful good yarn. If you got all that from them letters I got to learn readin."

Tom came into the cabin. "Your wagon be fixed, ma'am."

"Everybody to the table," called Nancy, putting on a tureen of stew. "Take bowls and pitch in."

It did not take long for the hungry group to eat. The guests said good-bye, and the Lincolns watched them walk down the lane.

"Pa!" Abe's voice had a new ring as he drew himself up as tall as possible. "Next week I want to go to school."

"What for?" Tom reared back.

"To learn readin'."

"Why?"

No Luck for Lincoln

"Well . . . ahh . . ." Abe cast about in his mind for a reason his father might accept. "Well, so I can read the Good Book."

"I can learn you verses."

Abe shifted. "How you read ain't good enough."

His father's brows drew together. "Be you saying I can't read? You hear me read that Good Book every night."

"But each time you read the verses different."

"Well, I get them close enough."

"No. I want to read them myself."

"Let him try school," pleaded Nancy. "He be five years."

"It ain't safe going through the woods. He get lost," said Tom.

"Pa, I know the way to the Allen farm. Me and you went there when you cut windows in their barn."

"But we rode Old Limpy. On foot, trails be different."

"I won't get lost. Let me try it."

Tom Lincoln scowled. Surrender was hard. "Well, if you go to blab school, first you got to do your chores."

"I do them." Abe jerked his head in emphasis.

His father shrugged and started out the door.

"Tom, wait!" called Nancy. "Can Sarah go, too?"

"A girl in school? We ain't that toplofty."

A Broken Wagon

Nancy's chin lifted and her words rolled out like heavy boulders as she went on.

"Two young-uns be safer in the woods than one. If a rattler bit one the other could . . ."

"Won't neither of them last a week," he cut in and stalked from the cabin.

CHAPTER 6

Blab School

The Monday morning sun was barely peeping over the pine tops when Abe and Sarah kissed their mother good-bye. Abe's face glowed with excitement which irked his father.

"A son of mine in blab school!" Tom twisted his mouth.

"It be called ABC school," corrected Nancy. "Bye."

The two started down the lane. Abe had a bouncy step because he wore not only his leather pants but also moccasins that his mother had sewed with her new needles. He swung a pail of corn cakes for their lunch. Sarah half trotted to keep up with him.

Although neither had ever been inside a school, they knew from listening to grown-ups that classes started early and lasted till late afternoon. Long hours were necessary because schoolmasters were often drifters. Seldom did one stay more than a few weeks. Since the parents paid his salary they wanted to get as much

44

"learnin'" from him as was possible before he left.

Abe and Sarah had no trouble finding the schoolhouse on the Allen farm. The building had been placed on the slope of a knoll. The rear end rested on the ground and the front was on upturned logs. Underneath, the Allen hogs rested in the shade.

As the two children approached the schoolhouse they heard the students inside reading out loud.

"Do we just walk in?" asked Sarah.

"Reckon so."

They went up the front steps and halted in the doorway. At the far end a fireplace glowed with coals to take the chill off the musty air. The cabin had the luxury of windows, made by hacking out parts of the logs and fastening in oiled paper. The floor was of logs split lengthwise commonly called puncheons.

Abe sneezed as he caught the minty odor of pennyroyal stalks that littered the floor. He knew they were used to kill fleas and vermin crawling up from the pigsty below.

After a moment Mister Riney motioned for Abe and Sarah to come forward and sit on a puncheon bench. They lowered themselves with care as puncheons often had splinters. Other pupils twisted to watch and listen.

"You be the Lincolns I heard were coming? Can you read?"

"No, sir," replied Abe. "But I aim to catch on fast."

45

No Luck for Lincoln

"Good. I don't want bosh-heads. Here's a horn-book. You two use it together."

Abe took the hornbook, which was only a wooden paddle with the alphabet painted on the broad flat end. After a moment the master spoke again.

"Since you got no slates, I'll loan you each one."

Abe accepted the slates with pencils tied to them and passed one to his sister.

"Now you two get busy and copy the ABCs on your slates. Say them out loud as you write."

"Yes, sir."

Brother and sister worked until the master rang a cowbell for lunch. At once the big boys bounded out the door and down the steps into the yard. Though Abe and Sarah followed nobody spoke to them. They sat alone on a log and ate their corn cakes. When other students finished eating, they spied a turtle crawling from a bank.

"Hey, fellers," called a tall boy, "let's see how fast the critter can run."

"Yeah," agreed the biggest boy. "I'll get some coals."

Abe watched him dash up the steps into the room. In a moment he came out with a small shovel of glowing red coals. To Abe's horror the boy put the coals on the turtle's shell. Nobody was prepared for the new pupil charging forward to kick off the coals. Abe's gray eyes glistened with rage as he faced the boys.

No Luck for Lincoln

The tall boy came forward, his chin at a cocky angle as he spoke.

"Want me to put you in your place?" He showed his fists.

Abe squared his shoulders. "I ain't been swinging an ax for nothing." He showed his own hands hard with muscles.

At that moment Master Riney appeared in the doorway. He leaped down the steps and elbowed into the circle of boys.

"Who started this fight?" he demanded.

"Him." The boys pointed to Abe.

Master Riney took a step toward Abe. "I won't have fighting. Say you're sorry."

"Sir, I done right. When I done right, I be not sorry."

"Then it's the dunce for you."

Taking Abe by his hair, Master Riney marched him into the schoolhouse. Dropping him onto a stool, the teacher put a tall cone-shaped hat on his head. Other students came in, snickered, and took seats. Soon classes went on with Abe listening.

The afternoon passed and the room grew dim.

"Time to go home," announced the Master.

The pupils bounded out, but Abe and Sarah waited.

"Sir!" Abe rose from his stool and removed his dunce cap. "Can I borrow the hornbook to take home tonight? I bring it back in the morning."

Master Riney hesitated. "How do I know you'll be

back? From what I hear of your Paw he's a man of peace. After he learns you been fighting he may not let you come again."

Abe stiffened. "Be you gonna tattle on me?"

"No."

"Then I ain't gonna tell neither. But I done right."

A smile touched the teacher's mouth. "Boy, you got good stuff in you. You can amount to something."

"I aim to, sir. Can I borrow the hornbook?"

"Sure. See you in the morning."

"I be here, sir."

CHAPTER 7

We Move?

By the time Abe and his sister reached their cabin twilight dew was in the air.

"Pa ain't back yet from Elizabethtown," said their mother. "Get your night chores done afore he gets here."

Grabbing an ax Abe ran out to chop a log the right size for the hearth. He had just dragged it into the cabin when he heard Old Limpy's hoofs.

In a few minutes Pa strode into the room. His dour face told that things in town had not gone well. He flung his coonskin cap onto the deer antlers then whirled to confront three pairs of anxious eyes.

"Put supper on! I be hungry as a bear." He splashed his hands in a bowl of water always kept near the door.

Sarah hurried to put on bowls and spoons while her mother filled a tureen with onion stew.

50

We Move?

Not till after grace did anyone speak. Tom broke the hush.

"Kentucky be going to the devil."

"Why?" asked Abe.

"There be no sense to their land titles." He ladled stew into each bowl. "Then that awful slavery. Soon there be more blacks in the state then whites."

"Does that matter?" asked Sarah.

"Matter! If them fellows revolted, us whites would get murdered in our beds."

All sat as if stunned. After a tense moment he went on. "In town folks call me a white hokey."

"Why?" asked Abe.

" 'Cause I don't own no slaves."

"Will you be buying one?" asked Sarah.

"Never!" His fist hit the table. "No Lincoln would be a slave. Nor own one. It be not Christian. Maybe we leave Kentucky."

"No, Tom." Nancy held out her hands. "We got our home here. Abe and Sarah be starting school."

"School! Bah! Kentucky be opening a school *just* for girls. A female seminary they call it. Such nonsense!"

"What be wrong in that kind of school?" asked Sarah.

Tom waved off the question and went on. "Elizabethtown be even opening a house just for books. A library, I thinks they call it. More nonsense! Maybe we best move."

51

No Luck for Lincoln

"Move?" Nancy leaned over the table. "I hope you ain't hankering to go to no wild place."

"I can't do nothing afore I sell this place."

After the meal Abe and Sarah took their places on stools for prayers. Abe tried to listen but his mind was casting about in alarm. Could he manage to finish school at the Allen farm? As from a distance he heard his father's voice.

"Off to bed, all of you. Tomorrow be a long day. At sunup I go to Elizabethtown."

Abe and his sister dragged out their mattresses and lay down.

For a long time Abe stared into the darkness. Pa might really move. And he wouldn't mind going into a wild place. That's what Ma was scared of. Abe clamped his lips. But then maybe Pa would not find anybody to buy their farm. Gradually Abe's muscles relaxed and he fell asleep.

The next morning Abe rolled onto his feet and looked around. Pa had gone. Abe reached for his hornbook and studied the alphabet. With his finger he pretended to write the letters. After doing his morning chores he and Sarah set out for school.

Schoolmaster Riney stayed only a few weeks. He gave his place to Caleb Hazel who claimed he was qualified to teach because he had once kept a tavern and could count enough to make change.

All went well until cold weather arrived. It made

walking slippery, and even with a scarf and coonskin cap Abe shivered. He put hickory bark into his shoes to keep his feet from freezing. January ended Abe's term of schooling.

Almost every morning Tom rode off to Elizabethtown.

"What you reckon he be up to?" Abe asked his sister.

For reply she merely shook her head.

The trips continued into spring. Then one evening Tom made an announcement.

"Since it be now the light of the moon tomorrow me and Abe will plant corn."

Nancy smiled. "That means we be not moving, don't it?"

Tom did not reply.

After the planting was finished Tom began his mysterious rides again. One twilight in May he arrived home in a dour mood. The trouble came out at the supper table.

"I been named surveyor for the part of the Cumberland Road in front of my land."

"Great!" Abe cried with pride. "I never knowed you could survey. That means you can cipher."

"Naw." Tom waved off the idea. "I be no surveyor. Them rascals give me the title to get me to repair the road."

"How much do it pay?" asked Nancy.

No Luck for Lincoln

"Nothing."

"You mean you do that work for nothing?" asked Abe.

"Nope. My job be to get men living along the road to do the work." He sniffed. "They will send their slaves. That means I got to be a slave boss." He shook his head and rose from the table. "I won't do that. Nope. I *won't*."

"How can you get out of it?" asked Abe.

"We be moving. Yep! Right now."

"Now!" Nancy reared back. "We can't move till you get in the crops you planted."

Tom pulled himself up to full height. "Tomorrow I ride off and sell this place. Then we move."

"We can't move," cried Nancy. "We got too many things."

"We leave most of this stuff." He flung out both arms.

"Oh, Tom, I can't give up . . ." Nancy's voice choked.

"We move soon as I sell."

Abe looked at the tears rolling from his mother's eyes. Some day he'd give her a house where she would never have to move, never have to give up the things she loved. Yep, he would.

CHAPTER 8

To the Big River

During the late summer and into the fall Abe spent the daylight hours carrying pumpkins and corn from the field. He stored them in the barn where deer could not reach them.

Autumn brought the chill of coming winter. Abe watched flocks of birds fly south. His father continued his mysterious rides.

"Where you reckon he goes?" Abe asked his mother.

She smiled. "With the good Lord giving us such a bountiful harvest I be sure he ain't planning to sell and move."

Then one twilight Tom bounded through the doorway with excitement in every line of his body.

"Well, I done it," he cried.

Abe and Sarah looked up from where they sat stringing bits of pumpkin to hang and dry.

"Done what, Pa?" blurted Abe.

No Luck for Lincoln

"Sold this place. Yep, I done it." He splashed his hands in the water bowl then took his place at the table. "Put on supper!"

Abe stared at his mother whose face had drained into a ghostly gray. After a moment she spoke in a weak whisper.

"How much did you get?"

"Twenty dollars and ten barrels of whiskey. Each be worth nigh thirty dollars. Now we move."

"Where to, Pa?" asked Sarah.

"I hear there be land in the Indiana Territory." Tom smacked his palms together. "We got to get some afore it be all took. We move right away."

"Listen to me, Tom Lincoln!" Nancy shook a ladle at him. "I ain't moving in the face of winter. No! Not till spring."

"Nancy!" Tom's body stiffened. "The Good Book say the man be the head of the family. You live where I say."

Nancy said no more. In a manner of despair she put a tureen of stew onto the table. Nobody said a word until after grace. Then Tom began to explain, an edge of adventure in his tone.

"Me and Abe will set out to find us a new place."

"When?" The boy's eyes brightened.

"Soon as we can build a raft to take us down the creek to the big river."

To the Big River

"River?" Abe blinked as excitement raced along his nerves. His father's love of adventure ran in his blood. He glanced at his mother, but she ate with head bent forward, shoulders sagging.

The room bristled with such tension that supper was a silent affair. For family prayers all sat stiffly on stools.

"Now, off to bed!" Pa said after his last amen.

Tom's enthusiasm was still high when he rose from the breakfast table after eating bacon and corn grits.

"Bundle up, Son. Me and you is going to build a raft."

They both mounted Old Limpy and rode off to a grove of poplars. Abe watched his father chop down several trees. After the side branches were hacked off, the horse dragged the trunks to a clearing on the bank of the creek. By working every day they soon had enough logs for a raft.

By the end of October the raft was finished. Tom and his son rolled some of the barrels of whiskey onto it and tied them securely with leather thongs.

"Pa, ain't this raft too big to go down the creek?" Abe asked.

"We can pole it along if we get stuck."

The next morning Abe helped his father load his tool chest onto their sledge which Old Limpy pulled to the raft.

No Luck for Lincoln

"Why do we need tools?" the boy asked.

"If the weather holds good I aim to put up a cabin."

"Just me and you build a cabin?"

"I'll get help. Tomorrow dawn we leave."

Although the morning was white with frost Abe and Tom bundled up for the trip. Without a word Nancy and Sarah put on shawls and followed them along the path to the raft. They watched Tom put on board his rifle and broad ax, while Abe carried his hatchet and several mallets. Then Tom kissed his wife.

"Soon as I get a new place I come for you."

She nodded and choked back tears. Abe kissed her, blinking rapidly, then he leaped onto the raft.

"Off we go!" shouted his father.

Abe picked up one pole, and his father took a heavier one. As long as Abe could see his mother he waved. He wondered if he would ever see her again. She looked so tired and frail. Could Sarah manage the cow and barn by herself? Had he chopped enough firewood to last till his return?

The raft moved along. Gradually the current increased as more streams joined the creek and the raft moved easier. All day they floated through a world that was new to Abe.

At dusk they tied up and went ashore to build a fire and eat their supper. They bedded down next to the barrels and covered themselves with bearskins. For a long time Abe listened to his father snore and to the water lapping against the raft. At last he fell asleep.

Dawn brought no sunrise. Instead, the sky wore gray clouds.

"No time to loaf," said Tom. "Let's push off."

The current seemed faster now as if in a hurry. On passing a point of jutting land, Abe saw a stretch of water that popped his eyes in amazement. In front of their raft flowed a river with a power that was frightening.

"Pa, be we going into that?" Abe pointed.

"First we tie up and get our bearings."

By using poles and oars, they managed to get the raft into a quiet place by the shore. Both jumped onto the land. Side by side they stood peering across the Ohio River.

"Indiana be on the other side," explained Tom.

"But that river be wild. I be scared," said Abe.

Tom strained to see a cove on the other side.

"Yep! Yonder be a boat landing." He nodded in satisfaction. "No doubt the owner runs a ferry. Let's look for a horn. We'll blow it and he'll come and get us."

For minutes they searched in vain for a horn hanging on a branch. Abe poked among the leaves thinking the horn might have fallen to the ground. Repeatedly Tom glared at the darkening sky then at the river. His expression told that he sensed danger. Also, the air had turned colder. Abe's teeth chattered. Finally Tom made a decision.

"We got to push for that boat landing."

"But, Pa, ain't that a whirlpool yonder?"

"Son, we got to take a chance. Either go or freeze to death here. I won't give up without a fight. Come, on, Boy!" He started toward the raft.

CHAPTER 9

A Whirlpool

The current seized the raft. In a few seconds it was bouncing as if to escape an unseen demon. The barrels strained against their leather ropes. Abe watched them wide-eyed. If they broke loose they might roll over him.

When his father tried to maneuver the rudder it broke. He grabbed up a long oar. Gradually they forced the raft from the center current. Abe glanced over his shoulder to see if the cove was near. What he saw stiffened him in horror.

"Pa! Pa! Whirlpool!"

The warning came too late. The swirling funnel sucked in the raft. There was the sound of splintering. Leather thongs snapped. The barrels banged together and began to roll. Abe jumped aside to avoid being crushed as the barrels toppled over the edge of the raft. Abe grabbed his father's heavy chest of tools as his only solid thing in a dizzy world. Round and

round whirled the raft. Then the thongs on the chest snapped and it plopped into the water. The twisting power of the whirlpool wrenched apart the logs.

"Jump!" yelled Abe's father.

Before Abe could obey he was slapped from the raft by the big oar. As if by the protection of a divine hand he landed on the rim of the whirlpool. In another instant he felt his father grab the collar of his jacket. Both floundered in the cold water trying to get a foothold on the muddy bottom. At last the powerful body of the older man was able to pull them both onto a shore, slippery with mud. Wind stung Abe's face. His clothing began to freeze. Snow fell on his head.

Stunned, Tom turned to stare at the place where his raft had been. "Gone! Gone!" he cried as if not aware of the bitter cold. "Everything gone. Gone!"

"But we ain't gone," replied Abe. "Pa, we can't stay here."

The big man jerked to attention. "No. We got to find help." In the dim light he began looking for a trail.

He was a skilled woodsman and was able to locate a path.

"Stay close behind me!" he ordered over one shoulder.

While his father walked bent forward to follow a path among the trees, Abe looked from side to side, fear plain on his face. What if they met a bear and Pa

63

with no rifle? Suddenly his chin jerked up and he pointed.

"Look, Pa! A light."

"Where?" Tom halted.

"Yonder."

"Yep!" Tom's half frozen lips tried to smile. "A lamp in somebody's window. Praise God!" He broke into a run.

"Ain't that window got glass?" asked Abe.

"Yep. Rich folks no doubt. They'll put us up."

Tom hurried along a split-rail fence. Coming to a gate, he tried to read the letters then shook his head. "Well, it ain't no smallpox sign."

"Pa, the letters say POSEY." Abe read them with a feeling of pride in knowing his alphabet.

"Let's go in." Tom unlatched the gate.

As they stepped inside the enclosure a hound dog ran at them, barking. The noise alerted those in the cabin, and a man opened the door. He was huge with a heavy beard.

"Who be there?" he demanded.

"We be the Lincolns from Kentucky," Tom led into the light from the doorway.

"Land-agoshen! Come inside afore ye freeze your gizzards. How come ye out on such a night?"

"My raft broke up." Tom hurried toward a blazing log in the fireplace with Abe at his heels.

A Whirlpool

"Well, shed your wet duds." The elder Posey turned to his husky sons. "Give the folks dry things."

Although nothing fitted Abe, he was glad to put on big pants and a warm shirt. While his father told of their accident he stared around the room. Never had he seen such a grand cabin. Instead of a dirt floor this Posey home had a floor made of logs split lengthwise and smoothed. Over this luxury lay rugs of buffalo hides.

To Abe's surprise there were no three-legged stools. Everybody sat on chairs or a bench with a back.

After Mrs. Posey rang a bell the family found places at a long table. Abe waited for the blessing to be asked, but was astonished to see all the young men reach out to spoon food into their bowls.

"Pitch in, Billy-boy," the head of the family told Abe. Then to his father. "And you, Brother Lincoln, don't ye mourn over your barrels of whiskey. Me and my boys can no doubt pole them out. They'll float up somewhere along the shore."

"That be good. Hope you can fetch up my tool chest too."

"Sure thing."

Tom squirmed uneasily then spoke. "Brother Posey, I must be honest with you. I got no money to pay you."

"Pay me in corn whiskey."

Tom winced. "I reckon that be fair. Can I also rent a horse?"

"Can't spare it. Ye can use my mule."

"Good. And can you loan me a broadax?"

"Sure. And a smaller one for Billy-boy." He winked at Abe. "We run a tavern and can fix up a traveler with most everything. Even loan ye a rifle since yourn went down."

"I be obliged." Tom rose from the table. "And now since we be setting out at sunup, weather permitting, we best bed down." He twisted to look around the cabin.

"Men and boys to the loft." Father Posey indicated a ladder fastened to the log wall.

Abe turned to stare in amazement at the balcony. Never had he seen a house with one room on top of another. His thoughts were interrupted by his father's voice.

"We won't bother you none in the morning."

"Bother! I won't let nobody set out without a full belly." He crossed the room to scratch frost from the windowpane and look out. "Ye may be frozen in by sunup."

Abe grinned. He could not imagine a nicer place to be locked in by snow. He climbed up the ladder in a happy mood. The loft was warm because of the heat rising from the fireplace. He settled down on a cornhusk mattress and was asleep before his father started snoring.

CHAPTER 10

Abe Takes a Stand

T he next morning Abe awakened to discover that
he was the only one left in the loft. He hurried to
climb down the ladder fearing what his father would
say. With relief he found his father watching Mr. Posey
cut a map on a piece of shingle.

"There, Brother Lincoln!" He held out the shingle.
"Follow that road and it take ye to Peter Brooner's. He
can tell ye the best place to stake out a homestead."

While Tom Lincoln was studying the map, Abe
crossed the room and looked out the window. A light
snow sprinkled the ground but that would not keep Pa
from setting out for a new farm.

After a breakfast of ham, fried potatoes, and
pumpkin pie Abe and his father put on their jackets. As
Abe pulled a coonskin cap over his ears, his father
opened the front door. One of the Posey boys had just
arrived from the barn leading a mule hitched to a
sledge on which was tied the borrowed axes.

"I got no need of a sledge," said Tom.

"Sure ye do. Ye got to haul brush to make piles at the corners of the land ye want."

Tom frowned. "More expense." Then to his son. "Let's go. You can ride the mule. I'll walk ahead to follow the map."

Abe's face brightened. He trailed his father out the door.

"Just a minute!" called Mrs. Posey, hurrying from the cabin. "Here be some food. Ye may get hungry afore ye reach the Brooner's."

"Thank you, ma'am." Tom tied the package onto the sledge.

Good-byes were short because of the chill, and the Lincolns started on a trail pitted with deer hoofs. As minutes passed the sun softened the snow into slush.

"When do we eat?" Abe asked when the sun was overhead.

"We can't stop for that. You can eat. I don't know how far it be to Brooner's. Can't take no chance spending a night in these woods."

By late afternoon Abe spied a plume of smoke.

"Pa, I think we be coming to a cabin."

"Praise God! My feet be nigh froze."

As they rounded a clump of pines they saw a cabin.

"Pa, it got glass windows. Indiana folks must be rich."

After tying the mule to a tree, the two went to the

68

door. It was opened by a big man with a reddish beard. At his side stood a boy of about Abe's size.

"Howdy, folks," said the man. "I be Peter Brooner, best estray hunter in the land. Whatever animal ye lost I'll find it if them wolves ain't got it. Come in."

"We be the Lincolns," said Tom on entering. "I be wanting a homestead."

"Ahhh. A new neighbor. Welcome Brother Lincoln. This be my laddie, Allen." He patted the shoulder of a red-haired boy. "Yonder be my missus." He flung an arm to indicate a young woman lifting an iron lid from an oven on the hearth. "Maw! Put on two extra bowls."

"Glad to have ye for supper," said Mrs. Brooner.

Abe and his father sat down and stretched their feet toward the crackling hearth fire. Allen took a stool near Abe and the two boys grinned at each other.

Peter studied his guest. "So ye want a homestead. Land in Little Pigeon Creek be dear. Two dollars an acre. Can ye foot that high?"

"Reckon so after I sell my barrels of corn whiskey," replied Tom.

"Barrels?" Peter bolted upright. "Ye be a man of means. Ye want the best. Tomorrow me and Allen will lead ye to rich ground only a mile from Four Corners."

"Not tomorrow, Papa," spoke up Allen. "That be my day for the spelldown at school."

"School around here?" Abe leaned in excitement.

"Sure," Allen nodded. "Ye want to visit tomorrow?"

"Do I!"

"Tut, tut! No time for blab school. We got work to do."

"Brother Lincoln!" Peter's voice turned stern. "Our lads got to be smarter than us. Why ain't me and you asettin' in the White House in Washington? Why? Because we ain't got enough behind our foreheads." Then turning to Abe he went on. "Lad, what do ye want to do when you grow up?"

Abe felt his flesh prickle. From past experience he knew that it was not wise to speak against his father's opinions.

"Speak up, Laddie!"

"Well, sir, first I want to learn readin' and writin'."

"Hurrah for ye, Laddie. We got a fine school at Four Corners. It holds forth from autumn till snow gets knee deep."

Abe felt his blood race in happiness. Above the pounding of his heart he heard Peter Brooner speak to his son.

"Lad, go barn down the Lincoln animal afore Maw calls supper."

Much as Abe wanted to go with Allen for the joy of asking about the school, the warmth from the hearth felt so good on his cold legs that they would not move.

In a short time Allen returned and again sat beside Abe.

"You can spell words?" Abe asked.

"I think I be the best speller in school."

Abe gave a low whistle. "And you read and write?"

"I be pretty good at both. I got to be good."

"Why?"

"Because I aim to be a general like General George Washington. I got to be able to write orders for my men."

"Be there a war going on?" asked Abe.

"Oh, there always be a war somewhere. I'll find one."

Abe puzzled. "Do you use the Good Book to learn readin'?"

"Mostly I work on my own book," said Allen.

"Yourn? You got a book?"

"Sure. I show you." Allen rose and took a volume from a shelf. "There!" He handed it to his guest.

Abe examined the words on the front page. "What do them letters say?"

"Oh, it be a story about Robinson Crusoe who gets shipwrecked among savages who want to cook and eat him."

Abe gasped and turned the pages. "There be exciting things in books. I aim to learn readin' powerful fast."

"Will your Pa let you go to school?"

Abe's mouth set in a hard line. "I be going to learn somehow."

71

CHAPTER 11

The Half-Face Camp

T he evening passed quickly and the guests climbed to the loft to sleep. An aroma of bacon awakened Abe, and he hurried down the ladder for breakfast. On finishing, he watched Allen bundle up for his walk to school.

"I hope you win the spelldown," Abe said.

"I will if I get the right words."

"Do you get something for winning?"

"Yeah. A new slate and pencil."

Abe's eyes suddenly sparkled as an idea exploded in his mind. "When you win can I have your old slate?"

Allen hesitated. "What you give me for it?"

Abe fidgeted. "Well . . .ahh . . .what you want?"

"Oh, I reckon six cents."

"I pay you soon as I can earn that much."

At that moment Peter Brooner started out the door with his rifle on his shoulder. Tom and the boys followed. Allen said good-bye and ran onto a path into

the woods. The others walked to the barn. Abe helped
hitch the mule to the sledge onto which Tom tied a pail
of food.

"Abe ride the mule and we walk ahead," said Peter.

A pale yellow sun shone through the bare branches
and started to melt the remainder of the snow. After
plodding awhile Peter halted and studied each side of
the road.

"This be the place. I remember that," he said. "First
we hack us a path, then we can eat." He pointed to a
tangle of vines.

"Through them brambles?" gasped Abe.

"Sure. We can do it."

"I go first," said Peter, "as I know the way. The
going be not easy." Then to Abe. "Laddie, me and
your Paw will chop away the big stuff and ye hatchet
off what we miss. We got to make a trail wide enough
for the sledge."

As the men swung their axes Abe wondered if they
could ever get through the vines. A damp odor from a
deep carpet of leaves reached his nose.

At last they came from the woods onto a meadow.
From its center rose a knoll like a giant fist.

"That be the place!" cried Tom Lincoln in
excitement.

Peter glanced around. "I see no signs of homestead-
ing. Let's eat and then heap brush at the corners of
what ye want." After dinner Peter said to Abe, "Start

chopping, Laddie. Me and your Paw will step it off.''

Abe not only chopped but also helped tie bundles of twigs with wild grapevines. These were loaded onto the sledge, and the mule pulled them to the corners.

Hours dragged by. Finally shadows inched from the woods.

"Now we best root for home," said Peter.

Abe tried to hide his joy in being allowed to ride the mule. Every part of his body ached. He wondered how the two men had enough energy to talk.

"I cannot help ye tomorrow," announced Peter.

"We will manage," replied Tom. "Abe be strong for his age.''

Abe felt pride surge through his muscles. If he did a man's work surely his father would pay him. Thoughts of writing shortened the trip back to the Brooner house.

At the supper table Allen showed the new slate he had won at the spelling contest. Peter tried writing his name on it and then passed it to Tom Lincoln. Abe watched his father make a few marks.

"That be me." Tom tried to chuckle.

Abe turned his attention to the old slate. The small crack in a corner did not bother him. This was a bargain at six cents. He must have it. His jaws clamped in determination.

"Pa!" Abe began as they climbed to the loft to sleep. "I need six cents. Will you pay me . . ?"

The Half-Face Camp

"Pay you," cut in his father. "I be feeding you and putting clothes on you. That be enough pay. Go to sleep."

Abe said no more. Though he tried to think of a way to earn six cents he soon fell asleep. The next thing he heard was his father calling him to get up.

Abe rolled onto his feet and followed his father down the ladder. The cabin was fragrant with the odor of frying sausage. In another moment he was at the table, and Mrs. Brooner gave him a stack of griddle cakes.

When Abe had eaten all he could hold his father sent him to bring the mule and sledge. Without a word he went out the door. The patches of snow had melted, leaving the ground dark and moist. In the barn he hitched the mule to the sledge still loaded with tools and led the animal to the cabin. His father came out with a pail of lunch. In silence they started up the trail, Tom walking and Abe riding the mule.

They went up the path hacked the previous day, and Tom took the tools from the sledge.

"Now we build a half-face camp to prove this land be took."

The older man knew which small trees to chop down. Abe laced them together with vines. By dusk the two had a wall about ten feet long.

"Tomorrow we do another wall," Tom said.

At the Brooner's the tired Lincolns ate supper then went to bed.

No Luck for Lincoln

As Abe and his father were about to leave after breakfast the next morning Peter hurried from the cabin with a kettle of glowing coals.

"Hang this on the sledge," he said. "Use it to start a bonfire to warm ye."

Silently Abe and his father went to their homestead land. By late afternoon a second wall and part of a third were standing. The next day the third was finished, and a sort of roof put on with poles and boughs. The fourth side was mostly open. Tom stepped back to study the half-face cabin.

"Good job." His mouth stretched into a grin. "Tomorrow we go and fetch your Ma and Sarah."

"Fetch Ma!" Abe stiffened. "This ain't good enough. . . ."

"Young-un!" cut in Tom. "Settlers make do in half-face camps till they get a cabin built."

"But Ma be different. She's scared of wild critters. A bear could walk in this open side."

"Not when I keep a fire going day and night. Critters hate fire."

Abe shook his head. "Ma won't come when she finds out. . ."

"She'll come," broke in his father. "Now back to the Brooner's for the night."

Abe's lower lip jutted out but he said nothing.

Lost

That night Abe lay awake wondering how he could keep his mother from that half-face camp. When his father finally called him, he arose without a word and climbed down the ladder. He flopped onto a seat at the table, and Mrs. Brooner gave him breakfast.

"Wish you were going to school with me," Allen said.

"Me, too. I be there after we move."

"No blab school!" snapped his father. Then turning to his host, "Brother Brooner, I pay you if you help me put up my cabin."

"Glad to, both me and my laddie. But we take no pay for helping a neighbor put a roof over his head. Maybe the Posey boys will help too."

"Good. Today I go fetch my family."

After finishing breakfast, the Lincolns said goodbye. With the mule and the sledge they started down the road to the Posey farm. Abe rode the mule, his head bent forward in thought. The half-face camp haunted him. He frowned when his father's voice boomed out his favorite song, "Gimme That Old-Time Religion." Not until Abe smelled the manure did he realize they had reached the Posey barn.

"Anybody here?" called Tom at the door.

At once the elder Posey appeared and extended his hand. "Welcome, Brother Lincoln. I got good news for ye."

"What?"

"Your barrels floated up onto the shore. Me and my boys poled them out. We rolled them to the side of my barn. There they be." He pointed. "And not broke up."

"Praise be! What of my tool chest?"

"We hooked that up, too."

"Good! Can't thank you enough."

"Them be nice words, Brother Lincoln. How about some thanks I can feel with my fingers?"

"I told you I got no money yet."

"How about paying me with one barrel of whiskey?"

"One . . . ahh . . . one barrel? That be powerful steep charge. A man got to work nigh two months to earn the price of one barrel. You folks worked only. . . ?"

"Don't forget, sir, ye also be renting my rifle and axes. Not to mention my mule and sledge. What be

78

more, ye'll be needing them to go home for your family, won't ye?"

"I don't need the sledge. Got one at home."

"Well," continued Mr. Posey, "ye need me to ferry ye over the river, don't ye?"

Abe saw his father stiffen for a final haggle.

"Will you come over and fetch me and my family when I return?"

"Sure. Let me know when."

"How can I let you know?"

"My boys hang a horn on a tree. Ye blow. We come."

"I be depending on that. Take one barrel. Well, I better move along while the sky be blue."

"I call my boys." He banged on a pan.

In a few moments the Posey youths arrived. At once the barn came alive as oars and poles were taken from the walls. In a short time Abe was struggling to keep up with the single file moving down the path to the cove. He copied his father in leaping onto the flat-bottomed scow moored to a tree. Abe watched a young man blindfold the mule and lead it over a gangplank. As if they had done it a hundred times, the boys pushed from the cove with their long oars taking care to avoid the whirlpool. The scow glided out into the muddy current. Abe marveled at their skill and wondered if he could run a ferry.

On reaching the other side, Abe and his father

jumped onto the bank, then watched the young men lead the mule ashore.

"Now, Brother Posey!" Tom jerked his head. "By our deal you promise to come and ferry us back?"

"Ye blow the horn." He pointed to where one of his sons was fastening a horn onto a branch.

"I hope you hear it," added Tom.

"I got good hearing. Well, luck to ye. Bye."

Abe watched the scow push away. Suddenly he felt abandoned. There was no security now in his world. He twisted to look up the creek they planned to follow to find their home. Sharply he remembered the place where it divided. Would his father know which branch to take? The idea put a lump in Abe's throat. Suddenly he heard his father's voice.

"Let's get moving. We got to hack a path wide enough for our sledge coming back."

Abe stared at the thicket of bushes and vines. It looked like an endless stretch as far as he could see.

Tom led off using his heavy ax to chop the big branches, leaving the smaller ones for Abe to cut with his hatchet. All day Abe kept looking up the creek, hoping to see smoke from their cabin. Shadows grew darker. The blue sky turned to gray.

"Pa!" Abe had an anxious tone. "Be we lost?"

"Course not."

Abe looked at the mule clomping behind him. It didn't know enough to be scared.

80

CHAPTER 13

The Blackest Night

A be jerked around to hear his father's voice.
"We spend the night here. First, we build a bonfire."

Abe watched his father take a piece of flint from the saddlebag, then bring out a stick of steel. Next came the family powder horn. Again Tom spoke.

"Get me some dry leaves for kindling."

Finding leaves dry enough to catch fire was not easy. Everything was damp from the storm and also it was hard to see in the twilight. Abe clawed into sheltered places, hoping nothing would bite him. Little by little he made a pile of leaves.

After many tries his father finally had a fire going.

"We got to keep this alive till dawn," warned Tom.

"Yes, sir. We can take turns staying awake."

"Nope. I set guard. I may need to shoot."

Abe winced at the thought, then tied the mule where it could nibble withered grass. He scrambled together more leaves to form a bed beside the fire. When he lay down it was hard to keep his eyes closed. The forest had such spooky noises. In addition to the snapping flames he heard the breaking of branches as wild creatures prowled near by. Finally he went to sleep.

At dawn his father called him to put out the fire so they could start up the creek again. An hour passed. Two. The sun rose high overhead. The only thing to eat was wild nuts that the squirrels had not hidden.

"Drink a lot of water," said his father. "It'll make your inners feel full."

By night neither talked. Again Tom built a fire.

"Tonight we take turns on guard," he told his son.

Abe nodded. Secretly he wondered if his aching muscles would hold him sitting up. Suppose a bear came?

Whenever his eyelids drooped he stood up and stretched. At last a hint of daylight showed, and he awakened his father. Again they started hacking a trail. Abe felt that his hatchet was duller and his feet heavier. Then suddenly he halted.

"Pa! I think I smell bacon."

"Praise be!"

On going round a bend they found a path to their cabin. Abe leaped into a run. He pushed open the door.

"Thank heaven you be safe," cried his mother rushing to throw her arms about him and then around his father.

"We be plum starved," Abe said.

"Wash up while I fix you a meal."

Sitting at the table, Tom enthused over the homestead he had marked out in the Territory of Indiana. It was on a knoll and drainage was good so no water could settle into the cabin.

"Cabin?" Nancy blinked. "You already built a cabin?"

"It be only a half-face but. . . "

"Half-face!" Her spine stiffened. "That be a shed. You don't expect me and Sarah to live in a shed?"

"Only till I build a cabin."

"No, sir! I won't live in no such place."

Tom wagged a finger at her. "I be the head of the house. But don't worry. I build a cabin. Right away."

"Me and Sarah stay here till it be done."

"You can't do that."

"Why not?"

"You know I already sold this place."

Abe saw his mother's eyes flash. Never had he seen her so hurt. Abe and his father ate in silence. Nancy and Sarah just sat and watched. The air became so tense that Sarah went to her spinning wheel and began running it at a furious pace. At last Tom arose.

"I aim to leave here in two days. So start packing."

"Two days!" Nancy pulled to her feet.

"Yep, two. We got to move while the weather be good."

"But I can't do my chores and pack in that time."

"Not much to pack. We ain't taking nothing I can hammer together at the new place. No table, benches . . ."

"But I got to pack dishes, bedding, clothes, my loom, the spinning wheel." She flung out her arms to include the room.

For a moment Tom looked bewildered. "You know I can't carry all them trappings on the back of one mule."

"We got Old Limpy," reminded Abe.

"Ma and Sarah will ride her. Me and you got to walk."

"What about the cow?" asked Abe.

"She can carry stuff on her back."

Nancy collapsed onto a stool as if all energy had drained out of her. For a moment Abe studied her ghostly white face then alarm needled him to speak.

"Pa, can't you rent a wagon at Elizabethtown?"

"Money throwed away."

Abe frowned, then again turned to his father.

"Can't we load Ma's things onto our old sledge and let the mule pull it?" There was victory in his tone.

"Our sledge be rickety. Maybe it hold some things. Go fetch it! I'll fix a coop for the chickens."

Abe left the cabin. At the barn he cleared away the trash and examined the sledge. Although it was no

No Luck for Lincoln

bigger than two benches side by side and had rusty runners it was not broken. It could carry a lot of things.

By pushing and pulling, he managed to get it to the cabin doorway. When he went inside he halted in amazement. Ma and Sarah were shoving things into the center of the room.

"All them things to go?" he stammered.

Before his mother could reply Pa entered the room.

"You can't take all that." He vigorously shook his head. "The sledge has got to carry the chicken coop, a bin of corn, and my plow."

Nancy began to cry as he dragged away one item after another. Abe's face twisted in misery. Finally he spoke.

"Pa, can't we come back later for the farm things?"

Tom twisted his mouth. "Well . . . ahh . . . I reckon so." When Nancy broke into sobs he went on in a louder voice as if to salvage a degree of victory. "I will leave the plow if you agree to start as soon as I can load."

"When will that be?" Nancy demanded.

"By sunrise."

"You mean tomorrow?" she gasped.

"Yep."

"Can't you make it the next day?"

"Nope. My bunions be aching. That means bad weather be coming. We got to go in the morning." Then to Abe, "Drag them trappings outside. It be still

86

light enough for me to tie some of them onto the sledge." He strode out the door.

Abe moved to his mother's side and lowered his voice.

"Pa's bunions be usually right. Maybe we better go at dawn than get caught in the woods in a drizzle."

CHAPTER 14

Fangs

A be helped his father load the sledge until it was as high as his head. The last thing to go on was the spinning wheel. By dark all was packed except the kettles needed for supper.

When Sarah rang the supper gong, Pa came from the barn.

"I boarded up my hay so the deer can't eat it," he announced. "Later me and Abe will come back and get barn stuff."

After the evening meal Nancy set out her iron kettles.

"Can them go on the sledge?" She pointed. "I got to have them to cook at the new place."

"Sledge be full," Tom replied. "Them kettles got to hang on Old Limpy's neck."

"But, Pa!" protested Sarah. "Me and Ma is riding him."

"You can walk part of the time."

Fangs

"My shoes ain't good enough." She held up one foot.

He ignored the remark. "Off to bed everybody. We leave when the rooster crows."

The next morning the rooster was late because the sun did not break through the clouds to rouse him. A late start put Tom in a sour mood. He slung a saddlebag onto the back of the mule then tossed a bearskin over the back of the cow. He stepped back to inspect his moving-day parade.

"I go first to lead the mule pulling the sledge. Next come Old Limpy with Ma and Sarah. Sarah will hold the cow's rope."

"What about me?" asked Abe.

"You be the rear to make sure no varmint attacks the cow. Let's go." He boosted Ma and Sarah onto Old Limpy.

Abe let his gaze move over the cabin. His expression told that he did not want to leave it. This was home. Would Pa build them as nice a cabin in Indiana? But then, whatever the cabin, a school was near. Allen had said so.

"Off we go to our Promised Land," shouted Pa.

He led the mule onto a narrow path that was almost like a tunnel through the branches. Runners of the sledge grated over the brown earth then silenced on the carpet of wet leaves. After a few minutes his happiness burst out in "Gimme That Old-Time Religion."

Though all knew the hymn, nobody joined in the many verses. Apparently not missing their voices, Pa sang for father, mother, sister, and all the saints. He was starting on the biblical characters when traveling grew rough. Roots nearly upset the sledge and Abe had to dash forward to steady it. Time and again Pa halted to hack off branches that threatened to tear off part of the load.

As they plunged deeper into the woods the trail grew darker. Above the treetops Abe spied gray clouds churning up from the horizon. Was a storm coming? Apparently his father noticed them, too, for he tried to coax the mule faster. This set the sledge creaking. The whole world took on an eerie atmosphere.

"Pa!" Abe suddenly called. "A wolverine behind me."

The word stood for savage terror. Although no larger than a dog the brownish animal had the courage of a lion. Its claws were as sharp as curved daggers and its fangs could bring down a deer many times its size. Now it evidently saw the cow.

When the cow smelled the animal she tried to escape. Abe grabbed her halter as she started into the shadowy brush. At this moment there was a blast from Tom's rifle. The wolverine collapsed onto the ground.

With caution the big man approached it to make sure it was dead. Then he lifted it by the tail.

"You gonna skin it?" asked Abe.

"No time." His father examined the carcass. "Good pelt. I give it to Brother Brooner to help pay him." He pushed the dead creature out of sight among things on the sledge.

"When do we reach the Brooner's?" Sarah's voice quivered from cold and fear.

Tom did not answer. Instead, he pulled the mule forward. "Giddap! We got to cross the river afore this storm breaks."

CHAPTER 15

Attack
from the Rear

By the time the Lincolns reached the river a drizzle was falling.

"Blow the horn!" ordered Tom.

Abe found the horn on a branch and blew a long blast. He strained to see across the river expecting the Posey men to be hustling to rescue them. Instead, there was no action at the boat landing.

"Blow again! Old man Posey promised to come."

Once more Abe blew with all his lung power. Then he listened for a shout from the other side. Nothing reached his ears.

"Gimme that horn! I'll wake the dead over there."

Tom blew it time after time. At last came a reply.

"They be coming," Abe told his mother.

He walked over to warm his hands on the cow. He looked at his mother on Old Limpy. Her face looked as white as the shawl covering her head.

When the Posey fellows arrived it was plain as they

leaped onto the shore that they were not in a good mood.

"Why did ye have to come in a storm?" one asked.

"I did not know it was coming," said Tom.

"Ye have a powerful lot of stuff to ferry."

It was a tight fit to get the cow and sledge onto the scow. Then in silence the young men poled and rowed over the river. At the boat landing Abe helped tie up the scow, then he and Sarah led the animals to the barn while Pa and Ma walked to the cabin. Mrs. Posey welcomed the Lincolns and set four extra plates for supper.

After supper sleeping became a problem. It was decided that Sarah and Nancy would bed down on bearskins in front of the hearth. Abe and his father climbed to the loft.

The next morning was gloomy with clouds. Tom lined up his procession. After saying good-bye to the Poseys he led the mule onto the trail. Nobody talked. The only sounds were the clomping of hoofs and creaking of the sledge. Abe kept watching for the Brooner cabin and sniffing to catch the odor of smoke from a chimney. Suddenly he shouted in alarm.

"Pa! Wolves be following us."

Tom tied the nervous mule which had caught the wild scent. Then Old Limpy reared up to escape.

"Sarah! Get off and hold her by the bridle," called Tom.

No Luck for Lincoln

At once she slid to the ground.

By the time Tom reached his son, the growling pack had surrounded the cow, which was struggling to get loose.

"I ain't got enough shots to get them all," Tom counted. "A wounded wolf be worse than a wolverine. If I throw them the wolverine they may leave us. Abe, go fetch it."

While Tom held the cow's rope, Abe pulled the carcass from the load. Then his father flung it as far as he could. At once the pack wheeled to pounce on a meal.

"Now we got to move fast." Tom boosted Sarah back onto Old Limpy. "Son, you lead the mule. Make it trot if you can. I'll guard the rear."

The procession reached the Brooner cabin before the wolves returned.

"Sister Brooner!" Tom began as they entered the door. "If you can give us a bite to eat we'll be off to our homestead."

"At this time of day!" Mrs. Brooner stood defiantly. "No, Brother Lincoln. Ye can't expect your missus and daughter to live in your half-face in this cold weather."

Tom reared upward. "Settlers always do that till they build their cabins. I'll keep a bonfire going day and night."

"Sir, your missus already has the shakes. Look at her! Let her and the girl stay here."

Tom frowned. "I need them to help me."

"Brother Lincoln!" cut in Peter Brooner. "Tomorrow I help ye build your cabin if ye let your missus and the girl stay here. I be a first-rate corner-man. What ye say?"

"How much you charge?"

"Us pioneers got to help each other. No charge."

"It be a deal."

"Now let's go unpack the sledge. Leave your house things in my barn till ye get your cabin done."

Abe trailed the men to the barn and all pitched in to unload the sledge.

"Now we put on the tools we need tomorrow," said Peter.

Abe helped tie on broadaxes, hatchets, mallets, and even a tool to slice wood for shingles.

"Now back to the cabin for supper," said Peter.

Tom was beaming. "Tomorrow I start my cabin. Praise be!"

CHAPTER 16

Never Again!

T he morning start was an exciting event. After his favorite breakfast of griddle cakes with lots of butter and syrup Abe brought Old Limpy and the sledge to the cabin door. Mrs. Brooner came out with a kettle of stew.

"Warm it over your bonfire," she explained.

Abe grinned. This day was going to be all right.

After a few minutes Peter Brooner came out with a kettle of live coals which he tied onto the sledge.

"This will start our fire," he said. "Now, Laddie, ye ride Old Limpy. Me and your Paw will walk ahead and plan the cabin."

Tom appeared and the three started through the woods.

When they arrived at the homestead the sledge was pulled into the open side of the half-face. While Abe unloaded it the men started the bonfire.

"First, we fell the trees," said Peter taking an ax.

Never Again!

Abe marveled at the way his father and Peter chopped down trees of the right thickness. As soon as one crashed to the ground Abe hacked off the branches. After each trunk was finished Peter notched the ends so it would stack into a wall.

"Abe, ye watch how I do this job. Some day ye may get money as a good corner-man."

By twilight the size of the cabin was marked out with ground logs. As twilight began to settle over the land all went home. For several more days logs were cut and notched. Then one evening at supper Peter Brooner made an announcement.

"Tomorrow the Posey boys are coming to help hoist the logs into place."

"Can I have a wood door?" asked Nancy.

"Not yet," replied her husband. "A bear hide will have to do till I can build a door."

Abe frowned. After he learned better to use Pa's tools he'd make her a wood door. Yep he would!

The Poseys came with all their muscles. As the walls grew higher Abe had another worry. Finally, he had to blurt it out.

"Ain't we going to have windows?"

"No time for them frills now," snapped his father. "We got to finish this place afore a snow comes."

Abe made no more requests. He simply worked. With the help of the Posey boys the walls and roof were

97

finally finished. Tom promised the boys another barrel of whiskey and they left.

"Ma will like this," Tom said admiring the cabin. "Tomorrow me and Abe will chink up between the logs."

"And I do the chimney," added Peter.

The next morning the three men set out for the homestead. After Abe filled the cracks as high as he could reach his father called him.

"Son, go toss another log on the bonfire at the half-face."

"Yes, sir."

Standing inside the half-face Abe heard sounds of wild turkeys. He peeked between the cracks of the shed. A family of gobblers was strutting from the woods. He caught his breath. The leader was the most beautiful bird he had ever seen. It surely weighed fifty pounds. As if to show off, the old gobbler spread its tail like a huge fan. The sun turned the feathers into shades of green and copper. The bird's red wattles hung on the bare blue skin of its neck. Its reddish legs stepped proudly forward as though to inspect the new structure on its knoll.

Abe's flesh prickled. Should he call his father? Any noise or motion could send the birds back into the woods. With his eyes Abe measured the bird and imagined it being roasted in the fireplace. There was always praise for a hunter bringing home prize meat.

Never Again!

Today it was his turn. Reaching for his father's rifle, he put the barrel to the crack. After taking aim he pulled the trigger. The female turkeys fled from their lord in panic.

Then Abe stood as if frozen in horror. One leg of the cock was broken and caused it to topple forward to the ground. From places in its body blood oozed over its glistening feathers. It tried to stand on one leg and strange sounds came from its throat. Abe wondered if they were from pain or were cries for help. The bird flapped its wings as though to lift into the safety of the air. But its energy was running from its wounds. The long proud neck could no longer hold upright.

Abe stared in anguish as the cock's head sank lower and lower still struggling to survive. Then, as if the mainspring of life had snapped, it sank onto a bed of nature's leaves.

Abe choked. Death! He had caused it. The bird had been enjoying life. Abe felt a retching in his throat. He had robbed a helpless creature of life. He leaned against the wall as misery tortured every nerve of mind and body. He felt sick all over.

Just then Abe's father and Peter Brooner, having heard the shot, came running into the the open shed.

"What happened?" Tom glanced around.

"I did it," Abe choked.

"Are you hurt?"

"No. He is." Abe pointed.

Never Again!

"A bear?" Grabbing the rifle, Tom ran outside. "Oh!" he gasped. Seeing the big bird, he went to it.

Abe staggered out in back of the shed and threw up. When he returned his father had dragged the gobbler to the safety behind the bonfire.

"Biggest bird I ever see," praised Peter Brooner. "We best take it home right now."

"Yep," agreed Tom. "Afore the wolves smell it."

The gobbler was tied onto the sledge and covered with a bearskin. After fastening on the tools and kettles, Peter turned to Abe.

"Get on Old Limpy, Laddie. Me and your Paw will walk."

As one in a sick dream Abe obeyed. He could not look at the sledge where the turkey lay dead. He kept his head turned away and occasionally leaned sideways to vomit. Two words kept burning across his mind as if on an endless track. "Never again! Never again! Never . . . !"

CHAPTER 17

Barn Raisin'

Abe had no appetite for supper. He merely stirred stew in his bowl while listening to talk at the table.

"Then it be settled." Peter clapped his hands. "Tomorrow I gallop to Four Corners and invite folks to a barn raisin'. Saturday be the best day."

"But I got no money to pay them," Tom scowled.

"Shucks! Nobody expects pay. All they want is food and liquor, plenty of both."

Tom shook his head. "I ain't got them things neither."

"Man alive! Ye got Abe's turkey. Tomorrow ye and the laddie can sledge over to Posey's and fetch back one of your barrels of . . . ahh . . . shall we say tonic?" He grinned.

Tom winced but said nothing.

As planned the household rose early. Then the two Lincolns hitched up Old Limpy and started for the

Barn Raisin'

Posey farm. Supper found them back at the Brooner table.

"I hope ye got the barrel," said Peter. "A heap of folks be coming."

"Is there enough tools for everybody?" asked Tom Lincoln.

"Every man brings his own tools."

Days slipped by. At last Saturday dawned. The sky was bright blue when Abe, his father, Peter Brooner, and Allen set off for the barn raisin' party. All had to walk since the sledge was packed high not only with the barrel of whiskey but also with baskets of roast turkey, potatoes, pumpkin pies, and corn pone. Wrapped in towels were plates, mugs, knives, forks, and spoons. On the end of the sledge Peter hung a kettle of live coals. Nancy, Sarah, and Mrs. Brooner waved from the cabin doorway.

On reaching the cabin, Tom and Peter soon had flames crackling in the cabin fireplace.

"Now we fix a table," said Peter.

All helped drag in logs that had been slit lengthwise. By laying them side by side with the flat part up, they made a table on which to put the food and dishes.

It was not long before the men began arriving. Some came in wagons; others rode horses. Some brought oxen to use in dragging logs to the side of the new barn. All greeted one another with the joy of a reunion. Abe puzzled. How could folks be so happy when they came to do hard work?

They kept coming. Never had Abe seen so many huge men. They reminded him of pictures of Samson in the family Bible. Then a lean man rode up, smoothed his white hair and dismounted. Why did he come to a barn raisin'? He was no taller than Sarah and much skinnier. Worse still, he leaned on a cane as he limped to a group of men. Abe managed to sneak over to Allen.

"Who be that?" Abe pointed.

"Captain O'Toole. Sometimes he comes to school and teaches us. He's got a thousand books."

"A thousand?" Abe's eyes widened. With so many maybe he would loan one. Abe began inching toward him.

Just then the voice of Peter Brooner boomed out.

"Up the axes, men. Let's raise Brother Lincoln's barn."

Grabbing their tools, the men clomped behind Peter into the forest. Abe hung back to try to talk to the Captain.

"Come on!" yelled Allen. "Get your hatchet. You got to help chop off the branches."

Abe leaped to catch up.

Soon the dull thud of metal on wood echoed among

the trees. After trunks fell and were trimmed an ox team dragged them to the barn site.

When the sun rode high overhead Peter called time to eat. All hands dropped their tools and raced for the cabin. They pushed inside and at once loaded plates with meat, baked potato, and corn pone. Then with a mug of liquor each sat on the floor.

Abe spied Captain O'Toole sitting on a stump near the hearth and sidled his way across the noisy room.

"Sir Captain! I hear you got a thousand books."

"Nope." The Captain's smile showed one front tooth. "I ain't got over nine hundred ninety-nine. Why?"

"Sir, with so many could you loan me one?"

The Captain squinted as he studied the lanky boy, then he spoke.

"Sonny, those books cost a lot of wampum. How will ye handle a book?"

Abe's pulse leaped. The Captain had not refused.

"Ahh . . . sir . . . most careful. Like an egg."

"Mmmm. Can you read, Sonny?"

Abe fidgeted. If he admitted he knew only a few words he would not get the book. If he lied, Pa was sure to find out and use his strap. Abe made his decision.

"Sir, as soon as we move into this cabin I aim to go to school and learn better."

No Luck for Lincoln

Before the Captain could reply Abe's father came up.

"What goes on here?" His tone implied suspicion.

Abe flung a pleading look to the Captain. Either he understood the mute appeal or else his military blood resented being quizzed by a man he did not rate as a superior officer.

"Nothing goes on." The Captain pulled to his feet and stood with the defiant manner of a fighting bantam. After a tense moment he went on in a softer tone. "Brother Lincoln, your missus turns out smacking good pies."

Tom nodded. Then to his son, "Let's get back on the job."

Abe trailed his father out the doorway.

After enough logs had been cut and hauled to the barn site several corner-men notched them. Then the huskiest fellows formed a line. When Peter shouted, "Heave!" each log was hoisted into position to form a wall.

By dusk the barn was up and roofed.

"Quitting time!" called Peter.

Again the workers rushed into the cabin to fill their mugs from the barrel. There was loud bantering and finally they mounted their wagons and horses.

"Don't try to drive," they called to one another. "You be too tipsy."

"My horse ain't had a drop. She get me home."

Barn Raisin'

Captain O'Toole was among the last to leave. While the other guests were talking to Tom Lincoln, the old soldier managed to whisper to Abe.

"I'll loan ye a first reader. Don't tell your Paw."

"I won't, sir," Abe beamed.

The Captain limped to his horse and Abe waved, grinning. He was one step nearer to learning to read.

CHAPTER 18

Fire!

F or some moments Abe stood with exciting thoughts tumbling through his mind. By studying a first reader at home he wouldn't be so dumb when he went to school.

At last everybody had left except the Brooners and Lincolns.

"We best go, too," said Tom. "After we rest on the Sabbath me and Abe go fetch my farm stuff."

"Your wife and Sarah can stay at our place till you get everything moved," said Peter.

"Can't thank you enough."

Several trips to the old farm were needed to move everything on the sledge and Old Limpy's back. At last all was stowed in the new barn. Tom and Abe ate their last meal with the Brooners.

The next morning Ma and Sarah put on their warmest clothes for the ride to the new cabin. They rode Old Limpy while Tom and Abe walked.

Fire!

Supper was cold fried chicken sent by Mrs. Brooner.

"At dawn I go get us a fat buck," Tom said.

He built a blazing fire in the fireplace. After a long evening prayer all bedded down for the night.

At daybreak Abe was awakened by a distant rifle shot. He sat up. Yep, Pa was off hunting. In a few minutes his father came through the doorway.

"I done it." He pointed outside. "Got us fresh meat."

"A fat buck?" asked Sarah.

"Nope. Never saw one. Got two fat rabbits. Tonight we have stew with dumplings."

"For that I need water," said Nancy.

"Have the young-uns fetch it from the spring."

"Where be the spring?" asked Abe.

Tom looked puzzled. "A spring has got to be near. Folks had water at the barn raisin'."

"No, Pa." Abe shook his head. "The men melted snow just as we done when we was building."

For a moment Tom blinked in shock. It was a blunder to build where there was no water. Then his self-confidence surged through his veins.

"We passed a spring as we came from the main trail."

"That be a far distance," reminded Abe.

"It won't kill you and Sarah to walk that far."

"But, Tom!" Nancy stepped forward, "We need more than a few buckets. Ye got to water the stock. And suppose we got a fire?"

109

Both Abe and his father stiffened in alarm. Every pioneer knew that a cabin fire meant disaster. Neighbors were too distant to help.

"Well, fetch some pails," Tom said. "I'll have to find a water hole real soon."

Without a word Abe and Sarah each took pails and went out. On the way back they stopped to rest.

"The road home be longer than the other way," she said.

"Maybe our feet be getting heavier."

By the time they made their last trip a light snow was falling.

"Supper be ready," said Ma.

Pa flung another log into the fireplace. At once flames darted up the chimney.

"The chimney works good," said Abe. "No smoke comes into the room."

After the meal Tom took down the Bible for evening prayer. His words were accompanied by crackling in the fireplace. At his final "amen" Abe spoke.

"Pa, I smell smoke."

"Maybe the wind blew it in the doorway."

Nancy looked around, then turned to Abe.

"Son, go give a look outside."

Throwing a deerhide over his head, Abe hurried out the door. The ground was covered with snow. He sniffed. The smoke was stronger. He went to the rear of the cabin then jerked to a halt. Although the lower part

Fire!

of the chimney had been built with stone the upper section was of sticks plastered together with mud. Abe's eyes popped in horror. Tongues of fire were eating on the part of the chimney above his reach. He dashed back to the room.

"Fire! Fire!"

Everyone jumped up and ran outside. All knew there was no use to try to get water.

"Quick!" yelled Tom. "Hand me snowballs."

Abe and Sarah scooped up chunks of snow and passed them to him. He stretched and slapped them onto the flames. Slowly the fire faded into wisps of smoke.

"All out!" he declared. "Go inside!"

At the doorway Abe shook the snowflakes from his clothing and bounded to warm his hands at the hearth.

"Pa, ain't there danger of the fire breaking out again?"

Tom nodded. "I mean to sit guard all night. I'll bank the logs so no more flames. Tomorrow I fix the chimney."

"Not tomorrow," corrected Nancy. "Tomorrow you should go to the store. I need a heap of things."

"First the chimney. Then to the store."

"Pa, can I go with you?" Abe had an odd hope in his tone. "I can help carry . . . "

"Nope," cut in his father, "I got another plan for you tomorrow. Now everybody to bed!"

111

No Luck for Lincoln

After Abe and Sarah lay down on their mattresses in front of the hearth she whispered to him.

"What plan you reckon Pa's got for you?"

Abe lifted his brows. "I got a plan, too."

"What?"

"I be going to that schoolhouse and get a book Captain O'Toole promised to loan me."

"Pa won't let you go."

"I be going."

CHAPTER 19

A Mystery Trip

Weeks of snow dragged by. Abe gave up ideas of getting to the schoolhouse. Gradually the cold weather lessened and spring came. The sunny days filled Abe's father with ambition.

"Today I ride to the village," he announced at breakfast.

"Can I go with you?" asked Abe, a sly gleam in his eyes.

"No. Today I go on business. Tomorrow, with luck, I take you. Maybe!"

Many times during the day Abe and Sarah guessed why their father went to the village. Was he buying something? Selling? It was a mystery. Then at dusk he returned, left Old Limpy at the barn, and bounded into the cabin singing.

"You must a been to a camp-meeting," said Nancy.

"Nope." He slung his jacket onto a peg on the wall. With a broad grin he joined the family at the supper

113

table. "The Lord smiled on us today," he went on after grace.

"What do that mean?" asked Abe.

"Well, Boy, tomorrow you go to work."

"Work? Every day I work."

"Yep. But after you finish your chores here you go to work for Farmer Crawford."

"Who is he?" demanded Nancy.

"Fine man. Rich." Then to Abe. "I told him you be a good worker. See you don't make me a liar."

Abe sat up straight. "What kind of work will I do?"

His father shrugged. "A little of everything. Chop brush. Hoe weeds. Split kindling. Maybe churn for the missus. It be different every day."

"Be this for pay?"

"Yep."

"How much?" Abe's face brightened.

"Twenty-five cents a day."

Abe drew a deep breath. That was a fortune. It meant that at least he could buy Allen's slate for six cents. Abe lifted his chin. Soon he could start practicing his ABCs and learn to write words. Tomorrow could not come quick enough.

Abe rose at the first gray of dawn and hustled through his barn chores. After breakfast his father announced that he was also going to the village.

"Pa, I can find the Crawford farm by myself."

A Mystery Trip

"I take you to make sure you don't go off somewhere else."

Abe nodded. Sneaking off to the schoolhouse was not going to be easy. But there was bound to be a way.

As the sun touched the treetops he and his father started riding Old Limpy through the woods. The air was fragrant with spring flowers.

After about an hour Tom turned into a maple-lined lane. Halting at the open doorway of a barn, both dismounted.

"Anybody here?" Tom shouted.

From behind a horse stall a bass voice answered. In another moment Josiah Crawford appeared. He was a huge fellow with gray rumpled hair and icy blue eyes.

"Howdy, Brother Lincoln."

"Howdy. I brought my boy as I promised on our deal."

Josiah jerked his chin and let his gaze move down and up the tall lean boy. Finally he spoke, "He ain't what I expected. Too skinnish for work."

"No, sir," Abe spoke up, "Pa teached me to work good."

Josiah cocked his head in doubt. "Well, I give ye a try."

"Thank you," Tom replied. "When you finish with him he knows the way home if it be afore dark."

"It will be."

After Tom left, Josiah motioned for Abe to follow

115

him to the house. "My missus needs help today," he said. "Not easy work. Maybe ye can't do it."

"Sir, for all that pay I can do a powerful lot."

When Abe entered the Crawford cabin he stood speechless in wonderment at its size. This must be what the dandies in Washington lived in. He glanced at the walls. All the chinks between the logs had been filled in. No cold drafts here. Not only did sunlight come through windows of glass but at the side of each window hung beautiful strips of cloth. On a mantel stood a tall box from which a tongue wagged back and forth saying, tick, tock, tick. Most wonderful of all was a row of books. If only he could read the titles. Suddenly he realized that a woman was handing him a pail of water, a rag, and scrub brush. She was plump with rosy cheeks.

"I want ye to scrub the floor."

"Yes, ma'am."

Abe looked down. Never had he stood on such an amazing floor. It was made of puncheon logs that had actually been shaved smooth. His mother would surely like this. His thoughts were broken by the voice of Mrs. Crawford.

"Start at yon corner."

"Yes, ma'am."

By noon Abe had half the floor scrubbed and wiped dry. Mrs. Crawford banged on a metal gong, and men clomped in from the fields. They swung their legs over

116

the benches beside a long table and began to eat and talk. Abe listened as he continued to work. Finally they finished and left.

"Now me and ye can eat," said Mrs. Crawford.

Abe was glad to rest and the chicken with dumplings were almost as good as his mother made.

"Sonny," began Mrs. Crawford in a motherly tone, "will ye be a farmer like your Paw?"

"No, ma'am. I got no hankering for that."

"Be ye lazy?"

"No, ma'am. I got no time to be lazy."

"Then what do ye aim to do when ye grow up?"

"I think I'll be president and take Ma to live in a fine cabin in Washington."

Mrs. Crawford threw back her head and laughed.

"A fine president ye'll make. I bet ye can't read."

"Ma'am, I aim to learn. Some day my chance will come."

"How can ye be so sure?"

"The Good Book says with God all things be possible. Don't that mean learning to read?"

"Maybe so. Well, finish your work so ye can start home while it be light. I don't want ye lost in the woods."

The food and rest gave Abe new energy. He worked faster as a plan took shape in his mind. He would buy Allen's slate. Then with the book from the Captain he could learn reading. When at last he went to school again he would not have to sit with the babies.

CHAPTER 20

The Worst Has Come

By midafternoon Abe finished the floor.
"Go tell my husband ye done a good job."
said Mrs. Crawford.

"Yes, ma'am."

Abe hurried to the barn where he found Mr.
Crawford cutting pumpkins to feed his animals.

"I be done, sir. And a good job."

"Fine. Come back tomorrow."

"Yes, sir. Can I have my pay for today?"

"Pay?" Mr. Crawford reared back. "Be ye twenty-one?"

"No, sir. But I done the work so I . . ."

"Sure ye worked but your Paw gets the pay till ye get twenty-one birthdays."

"Could I have just six cents?"

"No."

Abe swayed in shock. How could he buy Allen's slate if he never got any money?

The Worst Has Come

"Run along now," Mr. Crawford urged. "Get through the woods afore them night critters come out."

Abe stood for a moment as if debating something in his mind. Then he took a deep breath and lifted his chin as he spoke.

"Sir, be the schoolhouse near here?"

"In a field off the left fork of the road. Why?"

"I was just wondering. Bye, sir."

" Bye. See you in the morning."

Abe ran down the main road. At the fork he halted. Sure enough, there was a log cabin in a field. That had to be the schoolhouse. Only one horse was tied to the hitching bar. That meant school was out and nobody but the teacher remained. Hoping it was Captain O'Toole, Abe broke into a run. Finding the door partly open, he pushed it back. A young man looked up from his table cluttered with books and slates.

"Howdy, sir," Abe panted.

"Howdy to you." The man smiled. "Come in! Are you a new student?"

"Not yet, sir. I came to find Captain O'Toole."

"Oh, he moved to Washington. Can I help you?"

Abe shifted his weight not knowing what to do. Finally he spoke, a note of desperation in his tone.

"He was going to loan me a reader so I can study at home."

"Can't you come to school?" When there was no

answer the teacher went on. "Why can't . . you come
to school?"

"I got to work, sir."

"Mmmm." The teacher rose from his chair. "Yet
you want to study at home? Most unusual. Why?"

"To catch up, sir."

"Mmmm. I may have something to help you." He
began looking through the things on his table.

"Sir, I got no money to pay you. But I'll do work."

"Here!" The teacher held out a paper of spelling
words. "Study these. Practice writing them."

"On what, sir?" Abe's excited fingers took the
paper.

"I'll lend you a blackboard that Captain O'Toole
left." From a shelf he took down a smooth shingle
painted black. "And here is chalk, too."

"Oh, thanks. Let me sweep the room to pay you."

"No! One of my big boys does that for his fee."

"I'll take powerful good care of the blackboard and
this paper, sir."

The teacher nodded. "Can you write your name?"

"Well . . .ahh . . .not exactly, sir."

"Tell me your name and I'll write it on your
blackboard."

Abe gave his name and watched the teacher write it.
"So that means me," he whispered in awe.

"Practice copying it."

"I sure will."

The Worst Has Come

"Now hurry home, Abraham, before it gets dark."

Abe went outside. Already the sky had turned a heavy gray. With the paper rolled in one hand and the blackboard in the other he dashed into the woods.

Only his mother and sister were in the cabin when he entered. He looked around the room.

"Where be Pa?"

"He rode over to the Brooner's."

Grinning in relief, Abe held out the blackboard. "See them letters? They say Abraham Lincoln. Me! I be going to learn to write my name."

Sarah examined the blackboard, then a look of alarm tightened her expression as she spoke.

"You better not let Pa see this. He'll throw it into the fire."

Just then into the cabin came the sound of approaching hoofs.

"Here he comes!" warned Nancy.

Abe tucked the paper and blackboard under his mattress in a corner. Then he tried to put on a calm expression as he lowered himself onto a stool. In a few moments his father strode through the doorway. His grim manner told them that something had gone wrong.

"The worst has come." He wagged his head.

"What?" begged Abe.

"The milk-sick. It be around again."

Nancy gasped. Nothing terrified a community like the words milk-sick. That meant an illness for which there was no cure or medicine. It killed both young animals and humans. Folks believed the disease came from a field plant known as snakeroot. If a cow ate it, her milk carried the poison to her calf. Or to any person drinking the milk.

After an awed silence at the supper table Tom spoke with an edge of desperation in his voice.

"Tomorrow me and Sarah will go to the pasture and pull up any snakeroot plants. I ain't seen none yet."

"Suppose the cow already ate some?" asked Abe.

"We'll watch to see if her calf gets sick. And at prayers tonight we ask the Lord to protect us."

CHAPTER 21

Don't Come Back!

T he next morning after Sarah and her father set out for the pasture Abe put his bare feet on the path through the woods. He breathed deep with the excitement of a secret plan. If he worked fast at the Crawford's he might get home early. Then he could study before Pa arrived.

That day Abe's job was dropping seeds into holes dug by the hired men. Although his back ached from stooping he felt proud doing a man's work. At noon when the dinner gong sounded he went to the cabin.

Not knowing where to sit he waited. When the men took their places there was no vacant seat for him. He watched them gobble stew and slurp up mugs of corn whiskey that was considered necessary to strengthen them for the afternoon chores. As he fidgeted Mrs. Crawford came to him.

"Sit on yon stool, Sonny. I bring food and sillibub."

"Sillibub?" Abe grinned. "Thank you."

No Luck for Lincoln

He could hardly wait to sip the drink made of milk curdled with cider. It was a real treat.

Abe finished his meal while the men were still drinking and talking about the milk-sick. Leaving his stool, he went to the shelf of books and took down one after another. To his delight he found that he recognized a few letters and could guess at words by whispering the sounds of the letters. His fun was interrupted by the voice of Farmer Crawford.

"Back to work!"

On Friday Abe was working with Mr. Crawford in the barn when his father rode up on Old Limpy.

"Howdy!" he said. "I come to get my son's pay."

"My missus got it at the house." He gestured.

Tom rode to the house.

A month dragged by. Hot weather settled over the land. The heat was exhausting, and Abe could hardly pull his tired body off his mattress each morning. As he trudged through the forest his feet felt as heavy as boulders.

All day he hoed weeds with his head bent forward, an old hat giving some relief from the sun. At the noon meal the cabin reeked with the odor of sweaty bodies. Talk was about the milk-sick.

August melted off the calendar. September brought no cool breezes.

One afternoon Mr. Crawford called Abe to his workbench in the barn.

124

Don't Come Back!

"Boy, ye be lazy. Your Paw said he learned ye to work."

"He did, sir. But he ain't learned me to like it."

The older man put on a weary smile. "I reckon a lot of your energy is going to growing. Ye be taller than when ye came."

"Yes, I know I growed, sir, 'cause my pants be shorter."

"When I pay your Paw your wages he can buy you new pants."

"Not likely." Abe twisted his mouth.

"Don't come back tomorrow!"

Abe gasped. "You don't want me no more?"

"That be what I said. Bye."

Abe turned and started along the path home. It was hard to tell his family he had been axed out of a job. His shoulders drooped. Pa was going to be mad. But then he was not a man to give up if he lost a battle. No doubt on Monday Pa would ride to the village and find another job for his son. Yep, Pa liked that twenty-five cents in his pocket.

125

CHAPTER 22

Help! Quick!

When Abe reached home his bad news was lost in excitement over the arrival of his Uncle Thomas and Aunt Betsy Sparrow with their adopted son, Dennis Hanks. They had lived not far from the Lincolns in Kentucky. A sledge piled with their possessions stood in front of the cabin. It was still hitched to an old horse.

"We be startin' all over and need a place to stay till we can find us some land and get settled," said Uncle Thomas.

"Stay in our half-face," urged Tom Lincoln.

"Thanks. We do that." Uncle Thomas puffed on a pipe. "I hope to buy a farm near ye."

"Take your time," said Abe's father. "Summer in a half-face be cooler than in a cabin."

"Oh, I nigh forgot," spoke up Aunt Betsy. "We brung gifts for the young-uns." From a carpetbag she pulled a small object and put it into Abe's hands. "A

126

toy soldier," she beamed. "It be like them that fit for General Washington."

Abe's brows twitched as mixed emotions flitted over his face. A soldier! That stood for killing. From memory rose the vision of that beautiful turkey gobbler. Never could he forget how it struggled to live. No doubt fallen soldiers did that, too. Above his misery he heard his mother's voice.

"What do you say, dear?"

"Oh! Thank you, Aunt Betsy."

"Ye be welcome. And for Sarah we brung beads."

"Thank you." The girl put the string over her head and looked down at the pewter buttons. "They be beautiful."

Abe studied his sister. She was not pretending. She really liked her gift. But his! What good was a toy soldier? He walked across the room and stood it on the mantel. Sharply he wondered if he dared hide it. Then suddenly an idea jerked up his whole body. He would give it to Allen Brooner who wanted to be a general. No, not exactly *give* it. He would trade it for Allen's slate. That would be a fair deal for them both.

Before Abe could find a chance to ride over to the Brooners to see Allen, his father found him a job at the village. Abe was to help harvest pumpkins and shuck corn. Each night he was almost too tired to keep his eyes open for supper. Yet at dawn he had to start out again.

No Luck for Lincoln

Gradually, autumn brought cooler days. Pa even let him wear shoes. Then came snow and Abe's spirits sank. There was no chance now to get to the Brooners and trade for a slate.

"Your chance will come," whispered Sarah. "Just wait."

With spring he had to help his father plant. Each day he planned a speech he meant to say to his father about going to school. Weeks slipped by. By summer he had a job in the village. At last September turned maple leaves to gold. One afternoon he walked home determined to talk to his father that evening. Abe felt he could get in a little schooling before the snows came. He had just entered his cabin when Peter Brooner galloped up.

Abe rushed outside, followed by his mother. Fast horse hoofs meant only one thing, trouble.

"What be wrong?" asked Nancy.

"My missus." He panted. "Bad sick. Need help."

A shiver went up Abe's spine. Workers at the village said the milk-sick was going round again.

Just then Tom Lincoln hurried from the barn, and Peter repeated his news.

Nancy turned to her husband. "I must go. Sister Brooner took care of me when we moved. It be only Christian to . . ."

"No," cut in Tom. "She could have the . . ."

"I'll come," Nancy told Peter Brooner.

Help! Quick!

"God bless ye." Peter turned his horse toward the woods. "I ride for the doctor. If ye get there before me tell my laddie I be coming. Bye."

He spurred his tired animal, and Abe watched him vanish into the shadows of the trees.

CHAPTER 23

A Night Ride

For some moments the Lincolns stood as if stunned. Nancy was the first to break the spell.

"I'll pack a few things and go."

"No, Ma." Abe shook his head. "Milk-sick be around."

"I won't drink any milk there. Besides, I be gone only a day or two."

"No!" Tom stood in front of her. "I forbid . . ."

"Tom Lincoln! You know the Good Book says we must go unto them that be sick." She glanced at the dark sky. "I'll get my cures." Then to Abe, "Fetch me Old Limpy." She started toward the cabin.

"Just a minute!" Tom blocked her way. "If you go Abe must go with you."

"Why?"

"It ain't safe for a woman to be in the woods alone at night. Also, Abe must bring back the horse. Tonight!"

Nancy bristled. "You know it be not safe for a boy

and a lame animal in the forest after dark. Wolves attack the . . ."

"No more talk!" cut in Tom. "I need Old Limpy at dawn."

"What for?"

"To sledge my pumpkins from the field afore the deer eat them all."

Nancy had no argument against that. She knew that pumpkins were needed to feed livestock.

"All right," she agreed. "Abe, fetch Old Limpy. I get ready." Her skirts fluttered as she ran into the cabin.

After Abe brought the horse to the doorway she called to him inside.

"Dear, in going to help the sick it be nice to take something to perk them up. I be taking Mrs. Brooner a jar of honey. Find something for Allen. Maybe something you whittled."

Abe's eyes moved around the room then lingered on the mantel. A grin twitched his lips. Here was a chance to gain Allen's old slate. Making sure his mother was not watching, he took the soldier and tucked it inside his shirt. He waited while she tied a few things into a shawl then both hurried to the mounting block. Abe straddled the animal and Tom boosted Nancy behind him.

"Giddap!" Abe kicked the animal's ribs with his heels.

Even in the twilight he had no trouble guiding the horse to the Brooner cabin.

"I wonder why there be so many horses here," he said.

Together they started to the cabin. Abe listened. Why were so many voices inside? That seemed strange when a woman lay sick. His mother knocked. In a moment Peter opened the door.

"I came quick as I could," Nancy explained.

"Too late." Peter shook his head.

"You can't mean . . ?" Nancy swayed in shock.

Peter nodded, unable to speak. Both looked across the room where Mrs. Posey was dressing the body of Mrs. Brooner for burial.

"I'll go help her," murmured Nancy.

"Ye best not. Mrs. Posey say she done had milk-sick so can't get it no more."

Nancy's face turned white. "You mean it was really . . ?"

"Milk-sick. Ye best go home. It may be catching."

Abe could not take his gaze from Allen who sat on a stool near the hearth, his face bent into his hands. Abe's face lifted to Peter Brooner.

"Sir, can I give something to Allen?"

"I reckon ye can't catch it just doing that."

Abe crossed the room and leaned over his friend.

"I brung you something. Put out your hand."

When Allen obeyed Abe pressed the soldier into fingers damp from tears. Though Allen tried to

mumble his thanks it sounded more like the cry of a wounded animal.

Neither Abe nor his mother held back their tears as they stumbled through the dusk to Old Limpy. A golden moon had risen above the treetops and eerie fingers of light poked down between the branches. The loudest noise was the lame animal's hoofs.

Abe held the reins loosely, sensing that the horse knew the way home better than he did. As the animal came into the clearing of the Lincoln cabin, Abe saw a lantern hanging outside the door. A prickling went over his flesh. Pa never hung out a lantern unless there was trouble.

By the time Old Limpy reached the mounting block the clomp of her hoofs brought Tom out the doorway.

"What be wrong?" Abe bounded to the ground.

"Aunt Betsy."

"What happened to her?" Nancy slid from the horse.

"Uncle Thomas, too."

"What happened to them?"

"They got the signs. White tongues. Vitals burnings. Dennis says not to come. Not yet."

Tom half carried Nancy into the cabin. Abe followed as if stunned. Surely the milk-sick could not take both Aunt Betsy and Uncle Thomas.

CHAPTER 24

Getting Ready

Before the week passed both Aunt Betsy and Uncle Thomas died from the milk-sick. Abe was trying to comfort his mother when his father came into the cabin.

"Son, come help me and Dennis do their coffins."

Abe tried to swallow to quiet his trembling throat, then followed his father to the barn. Since there were no metal nails Abe whittled pegs to hold the planks into boxes. He worked haunted by one horrible idea. Would he have to help put the cold bodies into their coffins?

He felt relieved when his father and Dennis did it. Then he was ordered to hitch Old Limpy to the sledge and go to the half-face camp. After helping lift the coffins onto the sledge, he led the horse to a nearby wooded knoll.

There was no ceremony, no music, no reading from the Bible. It was merely, "good-bye." After the grave was covered the mourners walked back to the Lincoln cabin.

"Dennis, you stay with us," Nancy told the bewildered boy.

"Thank you." He could only whisper.

Tom lost no time in finding jobs for both boys.

Autumn brought chilly days. One afternoon Abe hustled home from his job with more bounce in his cold feet. When he entered the cabin his mother was stirring a kettle of stew. After glancing around to make sure his father was not near, Abe spoke.

"Guess what! An ABC school be starting. I got to go."

"You have to ask your Pa."

"I know what he'll say." Abe's lower lip rolled out. "No!"

"The father be the head of the house," replied Ma.

"But I made up my mind." Abe stood with feet apart in an attitude of defiance. "I won't spend my life grubbing and hoeing. I want to know what be in books. I be going to school."

Nancy stood straight. "Can you pay for it?"

"I'll do work for the teacher."

"Your Pa won't never agree to that. Maybe I can weave some cloth to pay . . ."

"No! Ma you got enough to do."

A tired smile went over her face as she spoke. "I be lucky to have a son like you. Some day I be powerful proud of you."

Abe beamed. Her praise boosted his courage so that

at the supper table he dared announce that school was about to start.

"And I aim to go," he ended.

Tom twisted his mouth. "No blab school."

Abe slammed down his spoon. His stubborn blood ran hot in his young veins. His nostrils quivered with anger.

"Why can't I go?"

"Because I mean to learn you carpentry."

"I don't want to be a carpenter. I want to read words."

Tom leaned over the table with a look of victory on his face as he spoke. "Why you need readin' to build a barn?"

"I want to read bigger words than you do, Pa. Words in the Good Book like Shadrach, Meshach, and Abednego."

Tom caught his breath. Nobody was supposed to know how little he could read. After a stark silence he spoke. His manner betrayed a determination to win even if he had to compromise.

"Well! You can blab at school. But only till the snow gets deep."

Abe filled his own lungs with the joy of victory. His heart raced. At last he was going to school, providing the teacher would accept him. As from a distance he heard his father speak. "Afore you trot off to blab you must do barn chores."

137

"I will."

At evening prayers Abe did not hear his father stumble over verses. The young mind was on school. He would catch up. Yep, he would. Tomorrow he was going to a real school.

CHAPTER 25

A Hint of the Future

At the next sunrise Abe's father thought of a dozen jobs that had to be done at once. Abe finished one after another. Then snatching up his lunch pail, he ran through the woods.

As he approached the log schoolhouse he heard a bell. Suddenly he felt nervous and scared. He slowed to listen. All noise of play had ceased. Classes had started. He was late. Would the teacher let him in?

When he appeared in the doorway the students were settling onto their benches. He waited, not knowing what to do. Then the teacher, a tall man with the muscular poise of a panther, came to the door.

"I am Andrew Crawford." He took the newcomer's hand and led him to the front of the room. "And you are . . ."

"Abe Lincoln, sir."

"Glad to have you here." Then turning he spoke to

No Luck for Lincoln

the class. "I introduce our new member, Mr. Abraham Lincoln."

A flush of embarrassment surged up Abe's throat as all eyes focused on him. He swallowed and looked over the faces. After another minute the teacher assigned him to a place on a bench.

"Now, class," Mr. Crawford went on, "today we are again going over the lesson in what we call social grace. It is necessary that you learn this because some day one of you might be invited to Washington to meet the President." A titter went over the room but the teacher went on. "Unless you know how to behave, people may dub you a barnyard bumpkin. You don't want that, do you?"

Abe replied louder than the others, "NO!"

Each boy had to take a turn going outside and knocking on the door. Another pupil opened it and introduced the guest. All except Abe snickered as though the whole lesson was a joke.

At lunchtime Abe did not rush out with the others into the yard. Instead, he made a deal with the teacher to work to pay for his lessons.

After the class ended in the afternoon, Abe hurried home. As he started to tell his mother what he had learned his father strode through the doorway.

"Well, what did you blab today?" He made a wry face.

"We had a lesson on social grace."

140

A Hint of the Future

"What be that?"

"I'll show you."

Abe had Sarah go outside and knock on the doorway. Then he pretended to open the door and introduce her as Miss Sarah Lincoln to Mr. and Mrs. Tom Lincoln. At once his father threw back his head and roared with laughter. Finally he calmed down enough to speak.

"That be the silliest stuff I ever see. Nonsense!"

"But, Pa, that be the way folks act at the capital."

"That don't concern you none. What chance had a country clod like you ever going to Washington?" His father sniffed. "I promised you could go to blab school and I ain't one to break my word. But come the first snow, you get down to living by work and tools and not social grace."

CHAPTER 26

The Chariot Be Coming

Abe continued school. Each morning he hustled along the frosty path to the schoolhouse so happy he forgot his cold bare feet. At the end of each day on the way home he practiced spelling out loud. Later, after supper, he sat by the fireplace and with a stick of charcoal scratched words onto the wooden shovel then scratched them off to write again.

Then came the day at school when he was chosen captain of a team for a spelling match. He was delighted. At last the boys had accepted him.

"How did you do?" asked his mother.

"Well, I wasn't the first to have to sit down."

All went fine at home and school until late September. Abe came home to find his mother lying on her bed.

"I be fine tomorrow," she tried to assure Abe. "Go help Sarah put on supper."

Abe put bowls on the table. As soon as his father

appeared they sat down. Abe could hardly eat for watching his mother.

"Can I sit up with her tonight?" he asked his father.

"No, I do that. You go to bed."

Abe obeyed but sleep was only in short spells. As soon as the room was light from sunrise he hurried to her bed. Pa had gone to the barn to care for the animals. His mother's feverish face told Abe that she was worse. "Water," she whispered. When he brought her a dipper from the water bucket he caught a glimpse of her tongue. White! He tried to hide his gasp. Surely Ma did not have this . . . He shot a quick glance at his sister. It was plain that she had not seen the awful sign. Mumbling an excuse to go fetch the milk, he ran to the barn.

"Pa, do you reckon Ma has the . . ?" His throat closed.

Tom nodded. "I fear the chariot of the Lord be coming." He put a bridle on Old Limpy.

Abe swayed. "What'll we do?"

"I ride to Peter Brooner's. Maybe he got medicine. You take care of Ma till I get back."

Abe watched him ride into the woods. Above his thumping heart, Abe heard his sister's voice calling in a scared tone. He hurried to meet her in the cabin doorway.

"Ma's hands are like ice," she whispered. "You think . . ?"

"Pa's gone for medicine." Abe went into the cabin.

No Luck for Lincoln

The two children hovered around the sickbed. When Abe caught the sound of hoofs, he dashed outside.

"You got medicine?" he asked his father.

"Ain't none." Tom bounded to the ground. "I even went to the doctor. Nothing he can do."

"But we got to do something." Abe shifted helplessly.

"I rode over to where Dennis be working and asked him to come. At once!"

"Dennis?" Abe puzzled. "But, Pa, he's got a live-in job. If he leaves he may lose it."

"But I need him." Then as if to banish the look of terror from his son's face he put on a softer tone. "I nigh forgot. Allen Brooner sent you something." Turning, Tom drew from his saddlebag an object wrapped in an old newspaper. "Here!"

Abe took the package and unwrapped it.

"A slate." He held it up. "Allen gave me his slate."

Tom made a wry face and started for the cabin with his son following. Sarah met them at the door.

"Ma's awful sick," she whispered.

"We can only pray," replied Tom.

As hours passed Abe realized that his mother was not going to get well. He watched her wince as pain stabbed her body. Then gradually an expression settled over her face. It showed that she could no longer struggle to live. Death was not an enemy but the only friend to ease her suffering.

144

The Chariot Be Coming

That evening Abe and Sarah sat on stools beside her bed, their eyes wide and faces drained of hope. Tom threw another log into the fireplace. When he came to the bed Nancy lifted her tired eyelids and a loving smile touched the corners of her mouth. Abe leaned forward to catch her faint whisper.

"I go to be with Jesus." Her cold fingers touched her son's hand. "Make yourself a somebody I be proud of." Her drowsy gaze moved to Sarah and Tom. "Bye-the-bye we be together in heaven."

Near midnight Abe saw her shallow breath finally stop. He sat as one turned to stone. His father's shoulders shook with grief. Sarah made no attempt to hide her sobbing. In the background of the room stood Dennis Hanks, choking sounds in his throat.

After a few minutes Tom Lincoln placed pennies on Nancy's eyelids to hold them shut. Then he opened the Bible and tried to read but only a few words came out. He closed the Book.

"Your Ma be in heaven. No more pain. She would want you young-uns to go to bed as always. We got much to do at sunup. I watch beside her tonight."

Abe and Sarah dragged their mattresses to the front of the hearth and lay down.

The next morning at the workbench in the barn Tom and Dennis cut planks for the coffin while Abe whittled pegs to serve as nails. By early afternoon the box was finished and put on the sledge. Old Limpy pulled it to the cabin doorway.

"You young-uns stay outside!" ordered Tom.

He and Dennis carried the coffin indoors. After a few minutes they appeared. The bulging muscles of Dennis's arm told Abe that the box was now heavy. He would never see his mother again.

The box was placed on the sledge and Dennis led the horse to the wooded knoll. Tom walked on one side of the coffin to steady it over rough ground. Abe walked on the other side, his hand also on the box.

The burial was merely lowering the coffin into a grave.

"All say the Lord's Prayer," said Tom.

With this over Tom and Dennis picked up shovels. Abe felt a numbness chill his body as each man flung dirt onto his mother's coffin. The pine box gave back a sort of muted cry and Sarah burst into loud crying. Abe turned away and wept into his hands.

At last there was a mound over the grave. Dennis had to return to his live-in job so he told each good-bye. For a few moments the three Lincolns stood alone in the silence of the forest. Then Tom looked into the tear-streaked faces of his son and daughter.

"The Good Book say we got to carry on the good fight." His tone quivered, "Ma would want us to do that, wouldn't she?"

For reply they could only nod and wipe their eyes.

No Luck for Lincoln

"Then we go home. You two sit on the sledge."

As in a dream Abe obeyed. He stared straight ahead, seeing nothing. His mind churned like a whirlpool. Ma wanted him to be a somebody. "Yep, Ma!" he vowed inwardly. "I be going to try. You going to be proud of me. Yep, you are!"

CHAPTER 27

A Strange Trip

At supper nobody could eat. The cabin seemed empty and cold despite the flames in the fireplace. Abe was glad when Pa sent them to bed.

During the night the October clouds rained. At dawn a few snowflakes were falling. Abe knew what that meant. The end of school till spring.

Dreary weeks dragged by. November weather gripped the land. Almost every day Abe had to do the barn chores alone, because Pa was off with his rifle to bring home fresh meat. Too often he returned with only a squirrel.

The thought of returning to school in the spring sustained Abe. He practiced writing in front of the hearth and waited. However with the first dandelion Pa wanted to start planting their crops. Abe scowled.

"Wait till summer," whispered his sister. "Then your school."

But after summer came the need to harvest the crops. No chance for school. Autumn turned the leaves red and gold. One morning in late November Abe's father spoke in a solemn voice.

"Today I go away on business."

"Be you gone long?" Abe thought of sneaking off to school.

"With luck I come back soon." Pa's face lighted.

"Afore you go," Sarah spoke up, "can you fetch us food stuff from the village? To cook I need . . ."

"No time," he cut in. "The sooner I go, the sooner I get back."

Abe blinked in amazement as his father stood in front of a bronze polished mirror and trimmed his beard. Then he brushed his clothing and wiped his boots. Finally he faced his children.

"Now I go. God be with you."

"Bye, Pa," they said together.

From the doorway they watched him ride away on Old Limpy.

"What business you reckon he be going on?" asked Sarah.

"Maybe to buy you a fittin' dress." Abe looked at his sister who now wore her mother's black dress since her own had worn out.

"You need clothes, too," she replied.

Abe looked down at himself. His linsey-woolsey shirt had been mended in many places. His ten-year-old legs had outgrown his pants.

"Yeah, I do look stove-in." He sighed. "I was

planning on getting to school while Pa be gone. I reckon I'd get laughed at. Maybe the teacher wouldn't want me in his class."

"Pa will bring us some fittin clothes," Sarah spoke with confidence. "And he be back in a few days."

For a week the two waited as they worked, listened, and watched. Each dusk they expected to hear the clomp of Old Limpy's hoofs.

A second week passed. No Pa. Their dried vension was vanishing. To fill up their stew, Sarah added corn and potatoes. Then she put in turnips. Gradually the meat was only slivers and the taste mostly imagination.

A third week dragged by. Both children kept busy trying to take care of themselves and the animals. At night they sank onto their mattresses in exhaustion.

At the end of the fourth week Sarah collapsed onto a stool and burst into tears.

"Look at us!" she wailed. "We be plain dirty. Our clothes stink and I ain't got no soap to wash them."

"Pa will surely come tomorrow," Abe replied.

"Always tomorrow! Suppose something has happened to him like to Ma. Maybe he ain't coming back."

For a long moment Abe sat as if carved out of wood. Then he lifted his chin. His words came out with the force of stones fired from a slingshot.

"If God can take care of a million Children of Israel in a desert he can look after two Lincolns in the woods. We ain't going to give up."

CHAPTER 28

A Big Surprise

O ne noon in early December as Abe was chinking up new cracks in the log wall he heard the thumping of many hoofs.

"That ain't Old Limpy," he told his sister.

Both ran to the doorway and halted. Abe's mouth dropped open in astonishment. What he saw was beyond his wildest imagination. A team of horses was pulling a covered wagon from the woods.

"Well, God sure do work in a big way," he muttered.

"That ain't God," cried Sarah, "it be our Pa."

"Yeah. And he got folks with him."

Instead of rushing out in greeting both children lingered in the shadowy doorway. Abe watched his father jump to the ground, then turn and lift down a woman from the high seat. At the same time from the rear of the wagon bounded three children, two girls and a boy.

No Luck for Lincoln

"Be they relations?" Sarah asked.

Before Abe replied he saw his father take the woman's hand and lead her to the cabin. At the entrance he halted, grinned at his flabbergasted children, then exploded his news. "Here be your new Ma."

A large-boned woman came forward. She wore all black even to the poke bonnet tied under her chin. For an embarrassed moment her gaze went over the boy and girl. Then she turned to the man at her side.

"Be these humans?"

Tom reared back. "They be my young-uns."

"Such clothes! Rags . . .filthy . . .dirty faces, un-combed hair . . .poor things." She took a step and put an arm about Abe's bony shoulders. "I think some of the clothes in the wagon will fit you, dear." Then to Sarah, "And some of my daughters' dresses will fit you." She hugged the girl.

Tom twisted uncomfortably, not being used to affection.

Sarah Bush Lincoln stepped through the doorway then stood still. Slowly an angry red crept up her throat and over her cheeks. Her gaze took in the cabin from the floor to the roof beams. Then she whirled to face her new husband.

"You told me you were a prosperous farmer with a fine home."

"What be wrong with this?" He flung out both arms.

A Big Surprise

"Wrong! Dirt floor. No windows."

Tom stiffened in fury at being scolded not only in front of his own children, but also in front of the other three who had entered the room. His mouth twitched with words he dared not utter to his bride. Finally he spoke in an attempted tenderness.

"My dear, soon I be making betterments in the cabin."

"Soon! Right away!" Her eyes flashed.

While Abe stared at his new mother she removed her mittens, coat, and bonnet. Then she studied the cabin again.

"Well, Tom!" She faced him. "This ain't how I expected to live but I took my vow and I'll do my best. We'll be needing more chairs. There be seven of us. I ain't brought enough."

"Chairs?" Tom scowled. "We got stools and benches."

"We need chairs!" repeated the new Mrs. Lincoln.

Though Tom's jaw clamped, he nodded in agreement. Then he took a step toward the door.

"Abe!" he called over his shoulder. "You and Sarah come help me unload the wagon."

The boy and girl left the room at his heels. They exchanged glances of amazement at what they began lifting from the wagon.

"What be this, Pa?" asked Abe.

"Don't you know a feather bed when you see one?"

"It be a cloud. Who sleeps on it?"

"Not you."

Then came two chairs and a table so highly polished it shone like glass. Abe's fingers stroked it to be sure it was wood. Next he lifted down wool blankets and boxes of knives, forks and dishes. The last to leave the wagon was a walnut bureau so heavy that Tom, Abe, and Sarah could hardly carry it.

"Take care of that!" warned Mrs. Lincoln as they brought it into the cabin. "It cost nigh forty dollars."

"Forty!" Tom placed it by a wall then stepped back to appraise it. "Such luxury be nigh wicked. We must sell it."

"No, indeed!" Mrs. Lincoln folded her arms across her ample bosom. "I want my . . .ahh . . .*our* children to grow up used to nice things."

For reply Tom left the cabin.

At once Mrs. Lincoln opened the bureau drawer and took out a linsey-woolsey shirt and buckskin pants. Then she crooked her finger to beckon Abe to her side.

"Son, I ain't going to try to take the place of your birth Ma, God rest her soul. But I mean to love you and do for you as for my own boy." She bent forward and kissed him.

Abe swallowed, overwhelmed with emotion. Not since his real mother died had he known affection.

"Thank you, ma'am," he managed to whisper.

"Son, wash up and put on these clothes." She hung

the shirt and pants over his arm. "They be no perfect fit, but they be better than what you got on."

"Thank you, ma'am."

When Abe returned to the cabin a grin stretched his lips.

"My goodness!" Mrs. Lincoln threw up both hands. "What a handsome new son I got. God is good to me."

"Me, too, ma'am. I mean Mom."

"Thank you, dear."

At this time Tom appeared in the doorway.

"Abe!" he called. "You and John come help me clean the hen house."

Abe and his new brother, John, followed down the path.

Not until dusk did the whole family gather again. They took places around the table, and Tom gave an extra long blessing. Abe sniffed the roasted ham.

Supper was an exciting event. At the close of the meal his new mother passed out rock candy.

"Now!" she began, "we must plan for months ahead."

"My dear wife!" Tom put on a righteous air, "The Good Book says we are to take no thought for the morrow for it will take care of itself."

"Well, my dear husband, let me ask you a question. In the fall don't you put food in the barn for the coming winter?"

157

Puzzled, he nodded and she went on. "So must we plan ahead."

Tom cocked his head in suspicion. "What you got in mind?"

"Schooling for our sons."

Tom flattened his palms on the table. "If God wanted that nonsense he would have said so in the Good Book."

"Sometimes he talks in answer to prayer. He told me we got to send our boys to school."

Tom frowned. "Suppose they don't want to go?"

Mrs. Lincoln looked into the wide eyes of Abe which seemed to say that his whole world depended on her answer. Gradually her lips lifted in the smile of a triumphant woman. Her voice had a tender yet steely softness.

"We'll decide that later."

"Good." Tom arose.

"Now," said Mrs. Lincoln, "while you girls do the dishes the boys will put down the mattresses."

Abe leaned toward his sister and whispered, "I be going to school. I be learning readin' and writin' and cipherin'."

"What'll you do with all that?"

He grinned. "I don't rightly know now. I reckon God will tell me." Abe jerked his head in emphasis. "And when he does tell me, I be ready."

Chronology

LINCOLN'S BOYHOOD	YEAR
Thomas Lincoln and Nancy Hanks marry.	1806
Daughter Sarah is born.	1807
Abraham Lincoln is born near Hodgenville, Ky.	1809
The Lincoln family moves to Knob Creek.	1811
Brother Thomas is born and dies.	1812
Abraham and Sarah attend school for brief time.	1815
The Lincoln family moves to Indiana.	1816
Nancy Hanks Lincoln, Abraham's mother, dies.	1818
Thomas Lincoln marries Sarah Bush Johnston and Abraham acquires a stepmother, Dec. 2.	1819

Books for Additional Reading

Bulla, Clyde Robert. *Lincoln's Birthday*. New York: Thomas Y. Crowell, 1965.

Cary, Barbara. *Meet Abraham Lincoln*. New York: Random House, 1965.

Daugherty, James. *Abraham Lincoln*. New York: Viking Press, 1943.

D'Aulaire, Ingri and Parin, Edgar. *Abraham Lincoln*. Garden City, N.Y.: Doubleday & Co., 1957.

Foster, Genevieve. *Abraham Lincoln: An Initial Biography*. New York: Charles Scribner's Sons, 1950.

Horgan, Paul. *Citizen of New Salem*. New York: Farrar, Straus & Giroux, 1961.

Judson, Clara Ingram. *Abraham Lincoln, Friend of the People*. Chicago: Follett Publishing Co., 1950.

McNeer, May and Ward, Lynd. *America's Abraham Lincoln*. Boston: Houghton Mifflin, 1957.

Miers, Earl Schenck and Angle, Paul M. *Abraham Lincoln in Peace and War*. New York: American Heritage Publishing Co., 1964.

Ostendorf, Lloyd. *Picture Story of Abraham Lincoln*. New York: Lothrop, Lee & Shepard, 1962.

Sandburg, Carl. *Lincoln Grows Up*. New York: Harcourt, Brace and Company, 1931.